A LIFE BEFORE

A novel by

JULIEN AYOTTE

This is a work of fiction. Names, characters, places and incidents are the products of the author's imagination or are used fictionally. Any resemblance to actual events, locales or persons, living or dead, is entirely coincidental.

Author Photo Credit: Glenn Ruga

ISBN: 1523417609

ISBN 13: 9781523417605

Library of Congress Control Number: 2016903382

CreateSpace Independent Publishing Platform

North Charleston, South Carolina

Also by Julien Ayotte

Flower of Heaven
Dangerous Bloodlines

This one's for you, Glenn

CHAPTER 1

When you visit the island of Maui in Hawaii, one of the most popular things to do is to drive the long, winding Hana Highway, a fifty-two mile stretch along Maui's northern shore. And once you reach Hana, population of about thirteen hundred, you gaze upon lush tropical forests and scenic coastlines.

Before the highway was built in 1926, and originally paved with gravel, visitors and residents had to either fly in from surrounding islands to a small airport or come in by boat. So, if you wanted a quiet place to live or hide, you could not find a more welcome spot. The climate, the remoteness, and the access to the ocean at your doorstep, they were all good reasons for Mike Strange to be here.

Mike's house was a small A-frame, a simple seaside home overlooking the Pacific, just a few houses past Charles

Lindberg's former vacation house in Kipahulu. Mike and his late wife, Susan, had honeymooned in Maui in 1988 and had driven their rental car on the Hana Highway as all good tourists do. The serene beauty, the many waterfalls along the way, and the unspoiled landscape in Hana immediately caught their eyes, and they swore they would retire there one day.

Susan's untimely death in 1989, at age twenty-seven, squashed those dreams. At the time, Mike was a very successful personal injury lawyer running his own firm in Providence, Rhode Island, with another office in Boston.

The Stranges lived in a plush neighborhood in Cumberland, about twelve miles from his Providence office, and life could not be better for Mike and Susan.

They had met at Northeastern University in Boston where Susan majored in elementary education and Mike attended law school. Both took the commuter train to Boston from the South Attleboro station near the Rhode Island line almost on a daily basis, and literally bumped into each other on the train as they made a dash for a rare empty seat.

"Please, Miss, allow me." Mike said to the young woman reaching the empty seat a tad too late.

"Thank you. I guess I'll need my sneakers the next time I try to outrun you," she said with a smile that would warm anyone's heart.

"Where are you headed?" Mike asked.

"I'm finishing my teaching degree at Northeastern," she answered.

"Wow, small world, I didn't think anyone else on this train went to Northeastern. I'm at the law school there," he replied.

They carried on the small talk all the way into Boston, and even walked toward the campus together. You would have thought they had known each other for months as the conversation between them ended only when they had to go to different classroom buildings.

"Will you be on the train tomorrow?" Mike asked.

"No, I have a three-day schedule, Monday, Wednesday, and Friday. I work at the Providence Public Library on Tuesdays, Thursdays, and Saturdays. My parents pay for the tuition, but I've got to do the rest myself," she said.

"Maybe I'll see you again on Wednesday then?" he replied eagerly. She smiled as they went their separate ways.

Susan Pennington was raised in Pawtucket, two streets from the home of the Red Sox farm team, while Mike hailed from Angell Road in Lincoln, a short distance from the greyhound track at Lincoln Downs. She was a quiet person who, in high school, had dated very little, preferring to help out as a volunteer at the local day care center after school. Her mother would pick her up each afternoon around five-thirty. She knew one day she would become an elementary school teacher. But for now, she was excited to be on the train on Wednesday.

Mike, a pretty good athlete in both high school and college, saw his dreams of becoming a professional baseball player go up in smoke following a rotator cuff injury in his junior year at Northeastern. That's when he decided to pursue practicing law for a living. His father had been a corporate lawyer for a large conglomerate in Providence until his retirement.

"Hello again, Susan. I thought for sure I'd see you wearing your sneakers today. I saved this seat for you anyway," as Mike pointed to the seat next to him as he removed his backpack from the adjoining empty seat.

"Are you available for lunch today?" he asked.

"I brought a lunch. But we can meet at the cafeteria if you want. My last class ends at eleven-fifty. I don't have another class until two," she answered.

Thus began a regular three-day a week meeting between the two of them until Mike showed up at the Providence Library on a Saturday.

"Oh, hi Mike, what are you doing here?" she asked in a surprised tone.

"How about dinner tonight after you're done here? We can walk over to the Gaslight on Pine Street. Then I'll drive you home after dinner, or we could do a movie," Mike greeted her with his characteristic smile.

Susan felt very comfortable in his company and her heart began to throb at his invitation.

"I don't know, Mike, my mom was going to pick me up and we were going for pizza on the way home. My dad's still on duty at the police station until eight."

"Oh, I see. Well, if you've got another date, we can always get a bite another day," he replied with a disappointed look on his face.

"Let me give her a call to see if we're still on. I'll be right back."

Susan left the reference desk and went into the office in the back room. She called her mother and explained the dilemma. Her mother had never heard Susan so excited about going out to dinner with someone. She had hoped that one day Susan would meet a man who would literally sweep her off her feet. Spending so much of her time by herself, her mother knew what to say to her at this moment.

"Mike, guess what, my mom isn't feeling so well this afternoon and was about to call me to cancel our pizza date. She's going to wait for my dad to come home later, and maybe they can have a late dinner together. With my dad's police schedule, they don't get to eat alone too often. So, we're on after all," she said with a beaming smile.

"Great, I'll be back at five."

Dinner at the Gaslight was perfect. Susan and Mike each ordered a glass of wine as they sat down. The restaurant was not yet busy, but the waiter mentioned to them the place would be mobbed by seven. Fortunately for them, they would likely be driving to the cinema on South Main Street by then. After the movie, Mike opened the door for Susan on the passenger side of his car, and Susan smiled. No one had ever done this to her before. As they approached her home in Pawtucket around nine, Susan was sorry the night was almost over.

Mike walked her to the front door of the house, kissed her on the cheek, and said, "I had a wonderful time, Susan, can we do this again?"

Susan's mother, Alice, heard the car doors closing in Mike's car. She and her husband, Ralph, were just clearing the dining room table after a leisurely rare dinner together. She peered out the window and saw Susan kissing Mike goodnight. Once Susan entered the room, Alice spoke.

"Hi, sweetie, how was your dinner and movie with Mike?"

"We really had a good time. He took me to the Gaslight on Pine Street in Providence, real nice. Then we went to a movie at the Cable Car Cinema."

"What does this Mike fella do, Susan?"

"He graduates from Northeastern Law School next May. We met on the train to Boston a few months ago. He lives on Angell Road in Lincoln. His father is a lawyer too in Providence."

"Are you going to see him again?"

"Probably on the train on Monday."

"That's not what I meant."

"I know what you mean, mom, and yes, I hope to date Mike again," Susan answered, her face blushing.

Her mother smiled. "Well, maybe we'll meet this Mike Strange someday. Stranger things have happened." All Susan could do was roll her eyes skyward.

When Mike graduated from law school in 1987, his first pursuit had been to sit for the bar exams in Boston and Providence as he sought to be admitted to practice in both states. After successfully passing both exams, he decided to open a personal injury practice in Providence, not really interested in corporate law, or wanting to become an associate in a local law firm. At first, he could not even afford to hire a secretary or a paralegal. But as time passed, and his case load increased, a few good settlements brought in enough for him to not only hire office personnel, but to hire an associate to work with him. By 1997, his practice had continued to grow and he opened a Boston office with two more associates. The Law Offices of Michael Strange became known throughout Southern New England as one of the top personal injury firms in the area.

Mike and Susan dated for nearly three years before he began his law practice and they decided to marry in 1988. They both did not want a big, elaborate wedding, so they eloped to Hawaii on what their parents all thought was simply a two-week vacation. The ceremony was held right on the beach in front of the Westin Maui Hotel where they were staying. While both of them knew they would get a lot of flak from the parents for the elopement when they returned home, Mike and Susan were willing to face the music and begin life as Mr. and Mrs. Strange without the fanfare that came with most weddings.

Their life together would be anything but uneventful and neither would have believed it would end so abruptly.

CHAPTER 2

"Hello, how can I help you," the voice answering the doorbell spoke to the visitor.

"Venture Cable, ma'am. We're experiencing some weird signals from this area and it's fouling up reception at a lot of houses in the neighborhood. I've checked our meters and your connection at the modem box may be causing it," said the aptly dressed man wearing a safety helmet and holster full of tools. "I was wondering if I could check the connection just to be sure."

Susan Strange had been relaxing on her back deck, reading a book when the doorbell rang. She was starting to enjoy her summer break from her elementary school classes which had just ended in late June.

"Sure, c'mon in, the cable box is downstairs in the basement, right around the corner there," she pointed in the direction past the kitchen in their modern six-room one level home in the Woodridge Estates. Susan and her husband Mike had bought the house on Burke Road in Cumberland, Rhode Island, the year before, in 1988, shortly after their elopement. They had no children yet but were planning a family, and Susan even thought she might be pregnant. She had not had her period for nearly two months.

The service man entered the front door and headed for the cellar stairs as he listened for the sound of the front door closing. In a split second, he turned her way, pulled out a gun with a silencer attached, and fired three shots at Susan. She fell to the floor motionless as the gunman put his two fingers on her neck to see if he could detect a pulse. Feeling none, the gunman unscrewed the silencer from the gun, tucked the gun under his jacket, and placed the silencer into the pocket of the jacket.

So as not to arouse suspicion from any neighbors, he waited several minutes before leaving. While he waited, he casually poured himself a glass of soda from the refrigerator and gulped it down. *All in a day's work,* he thought. He placed the empty glass on the kitchen counter and headed for the front door. He threw pictures to the floor which were on a small table behind the sofa, pushed the sofa a bit, and knocked down the same table as he left the house, the visor of his safety hat shielding his face from anyone who might look his way. He got into his Venture Cable panel truck and left the area as fast as he could.

Mike Strange was very nervous at his Providence law office that day. He had received threats on his life from someone and the threats included harm to his wife if he did not stop pursuing a case he had been working on. The

case involved a wrongful death claim by a widow whose husband had died of lung cancer in 1987 at age forty-seven.
Ironically, the man had never smoked, was an avid tennis
player, and had no previous medical condition. The widow
had asked Mike to handle her suit against Tate Builders for
intentional withholding of information about radon gas
levels in the condo they had bought in North Smithfield
from the contractor in 1982. The condominium complex
they lived in consisted of nearly three hundred one-level
and two-level units. In the last five years, twelve people in
the complex had been stricken with lung cancer, and none
of them were smokers. Recent unit buyers now had radon
tests done and discovered levels of 11 picocuries per liter
or higher. The acceptable level of radon gas considered to
be safe is 4 picocuries per liter or less. The State of Rhode
Island, at that time, did not require contractors to address
radon problems, and they were not required to mitigate
the levels to an acceptable limit. The homeowner was left
with the responsibility to get this done at his own expense,
sometimes for a cost as high as $500 just to install a pipe
going from under the basement floor to a motorized outdoor exhaust fan that sucked the gases into the atmosphere
at roof level, rendering the gases harmless.

Mike had reluctantly accepted the case but knew all too
well how difficult it would be to prove willful neglect by the
contractor. He would need verifiable proof that the contractor knew ahead of time of the existence of radon gas
in the condo units, and never revealed the information to
prospective buyers. He was preparing to investigate each of
the twelve deaths from the complex to determine if there
was a connection. He had already hired a radon specialist
to conduct tests at each of these units to see what the radon

levels were. The thought of a class action suit against Tate Builders crossed his mind.

"Damn it, why isn't she answering?" he yelled from his office. "I know you're there, Susan. Take off the headsets if you've got them on."

After several tries in fifteen minute intervals, Mike started to worry that something was wrong.

"Gordie, it's Mike. Do me a favor will you?" he asked. "I've been trying to reach Susan and she's not answering. She might be on the back deck reading and can't hear the phone, and I need to reach her."

"What's wrong, Mike, anything I can do to help?"

"No, it's nothing, but can you just walk over and see if she's there? She wasn't going anywhere, I don't think?"

"Sure, no problem. If she's home, I'll tell her to call you."

Gordon and Betty Landry had been neighbors across the street from the Stranges. They had moved in about the same time in 1988, and had two small children. Gordie handled mortgage closings for a private mortgage company and worked from home several days a week. Susan had taken a liking to both kids immediately and the two couples socialized together in the neighborhood several times a year.

Gordie, a tall, slim man, walked across the street and peered through the glass panel alongside the front door as he rang the doorbell.

No one answered. He stepped off the front porch and headed for the deck in the back yard of the property. No one was there, but he noticed a book and a bottle of water on the patio table near the back entrance. He climbed the steps to the deck and found the screened door unlocked.

"Hello, anybody home? Susan?"

As he continued into the house's family room, he did not notice anyone. He saw the crooked sofa, and once he made his way past it toward the front door, there was Susan's body lying on the floor in a pool of blood.

"Oh, my God!" he shouted.

He searched for a phone, found one on the end table near the sofa, and dialed 911.

"There's a woman lying in blood on the floor at 171 Burke Road in Cumberland. Hurry, please, I don't know if she is still alive. I think she has been shot."

Within minutes, a rescue vehicle was in front of the house and rushing into Susan's home. Right behind the rescue unit a police car sped up to the front of the house with lights flashing. Gordie called Mike at his office.

"Mike, I found Susan, but she's been shot. The rescue is here now. Please get here as fast as you can. I think they are taking her to Landmark Medical Center in Woonsocket."

"Damn it, damn it, I knew something bad was going to happen. I knew it," as he hung up the phone abruptly. He raced out of his office, down the elevator to the parking garage, and hurried toward Cumberland. Before he could reach Cumberland, his car phone rang loudly.

"Mike, they've rushed her to Landmark. You'd better go directly there. I'm on my way too. It's bad, Mike, real bad."

CHAPTER 3

As Mike neared Landmark Medical Center, perspiration running down his cheeks uncontrollably, he could see the red flashing lights from the rescue van parked in front of the emergency doors. He pulled into the first parking spot he found, rushed in, and made a bee line for the attendant at the front desk.

"Susan Strange, the woman who was just brought in here with gunshot wounds, where is she? Please?" he was frantic.

"Are you a relative, sir?" the attendant asked.

"Mike, they've taken her into surgery," Gordie yelled as he raced down the hallway when he eyed Mike at the front desk. "At first, they had no pulse, but one of the EMTs did CPR on her and the other zapped her twice with the paddles, and they got a pulse. They said it looked like three bullet holes in the stomach."

"Did she come to, Gordie, did she say anything?"

"No, they had her on a respirator when they left."

"Mr. Strange, I take it, you and your friend here can go into the lounge at the end of the hallway. As soon as there is news, someone will come there to tell you."

Mike and Gordie walked toward the lounge and Mike started ranting, "I'm going to get the bastard who did this, Gordie. I don't care how long it takes me. I've got a pretty good idea who's responsible."

Gordie was confused. "Why would somebody want to hurt Susan, Mike?"

"It's not Susan, Gordie. It's me they were sending a message to. It's this case I'm working on. Really big, and somebody might have to pay millions if they lose."

"But what does this have to do with hurting Susan?" Gordie yelled back.

"Jesus, Gordie, don't you get it? You go after somebody in my family so you can scare me away. It's somebody telling me this can happen to me too if I push on this case."

"Damn it, Mike, what kind of people are you dealing with here? Why not go after you first?"

"Because it would raise red flags everywhere, Gordie. Once the police connect the case I'm working on with the people involved, they would put these people on the top of the suspect list. This way, by going after Susan, it becomes a lot tougher to link the two. The police can say this was a house robbery gone badly, if Susan walked in on someone in the house."

"Mike, I thought you just did accidents and stuff, nothing criminal?"

"Most of the time, it's true. But this widow's husband died of lung cancer at forty-seven, never smoked, excellent shape, and ran a mortgage insurance business out of his condo unit. So, basically, he worked out of his basement office by himself most of the day. His wife was a secretary in Providence, and when she got home around six o'clock, he was already preparing dinner. Sounds like a nice guy."

"So, what happened?"

"The guy gets lung cancer and dies, and hardly was exposed to second-hand smoke or asbestos, nothing."

"But he's not the first non-smoker to die from lung cancer," Gordie chimed in.

"No, Gordie, that's true. But what about the other eleven who died from it too from the same condo complex in the last five years?" Mike's look was obvious.

"What the heck is that all about?" Gordie asked.

"I think it may be about radon gas in all those units coming through the basement cement floor. I think this whole condo complex is sitting on a ton of it. I've talked to at least fifty newer residents there, and they have all had radon tests which showed the level way too dangerous, and they have all installed mitigation systems to bring the radon level to acceptable limits. The older residents who have been there five or more years were never even aware of radon, except those who put their units up for sale. Buyers wanted radon tests done. I know this case I'm working on has something to do with this," Mike moaned.

Susan never recovered from surgery. Mike was told she had lost a considerable amount of blood before the paramedics arrived and the doctors in the operating room did everything they could to keep her alive. She was only twenty-seven years old, an only child of Detective Ralph Pennington and his wife, Alice. Ralph had been on the

Pawtucket police force for over twenty-five years and he himself had been shot in the line of duty in 1982 during a shootout in an attempted robbery at a local liquor store. So he knew all too well about gunshot wounds.

* * *

"Mike, after today, you and I are going to sit down and you're going to tell me what this case of yours is all about, understood?" Ralph whispered to Mike at the collation lunch on Saturday that day in June, 1989 at the Cantina de Salvo Restaurant following Susan's funeral at St. Joseph's Church in Cumberland.

"I know the Cumberland police are working on this, but I need to be involved."

"Ralph, I will tell you as much as I know right now, but there is a long way to go on this before I have enough proof for a motive. No one wants to get Susan's killer more than I do, and I will find whoever is responsible for this, no matter how long it takes."

"Somebody has to do a lot of your legwork on this, and it's going to include me. Are we clear on that? The department says I'm hands off because I'm too close to the victim, and because it happened in Cumberland, not Pawtucket. But what I do on my own time is my business."

This was more conversation than they had had for over a year. It wasn't that Mike did not get along just fine with his in-laws. It was his legal schedule and Ralph's police work which so often interfered with any get together. Telephone conversations between Susan and her mother were more frequent since Alice had a similar teaching schedule to Susan's. She was a psychology professor at Brown University in Providence and she and Susan managed to talk to each other at least twice a week.

On Sunday afternoon, Ralph pulled up in the driveway at Mike's home and rang the front doorbell. Mike was dressed in jeans and a t-shirt as he opened the front door. After the customary offer for a drink, both of them sat down in the family room.

"Radon gas, Ralph, I think this is about a huge condominium complex sitting on a ton of it. I think the contractor knew about it long before anything happened because of it, and the contractor never told anybody about it. People started buying units. The case I have is with a widow whose husband died from lung cancer at forty-seven, a non-smoker. Why the widow said this was unusual, Ralph, is because eleven other people who lived there have died from lung cancer in the past five years, and none of them ever smoked a cigarette," Mike began.

"I was starting to schedule interviews with the surviving spouses of those other people, but I haven't gotten too far yet. The law suit I was about to file was going to be against the builders and their insurance company, Mutual of New England. My paralegal, Bonnie Stevens, starts tomorrow with the most recent death before this one. That was a sixty-two year old guy who retired five years ago, spent his days working on his model train sets in an area in his basement, and was diagnosed with lung cancer in 1987 before he died in the fall of 1988. He lived alone after he and his former wife had divorced years ago, but he had a son who inherited the condo unit and sold it just last year," Mike continued.

"Here's the kicker, Ralph. The new buyers insisted on having a home inspection done before the sale, and it included a radon test. A radon level over four picocuries is considered dangerous and needs to be addressed by a mitigation system to get the rating back to less than four picocuries. The radon level on the test at this unit came in at nineteen picocuries, nearly five times the acceptable level. The son told me his father worked down there almost every day for several hours at a time for nearly five years before he died. Five years, Ralph."

"What's with this radon crap, Mike? I've never heard of this. Alice and I have lived in our house for nearly thirty years, but we never thought our cellar could be filled with poisonous gas. Where the hell does this come from?"

"There are pockets of these gases underground which can leak into your basement through cracks in your cement floor or where the walls meet the floor if the area is not sealed properly. It's not everywhere, Ralph, but if there happens to be a lot of ledge in the ground where your house sits, it is possible radon is there too. Once you know it is there, you can easily fix it by venting the gas through a pipe under your cellar floor into the atmosphere outside the house. But if the contractor knows that radon exists in your unit or house, he is supposed to tell you about it so you can get rid of it. If he doesn't tell you, and he knew about it, he could be found negligent and be liable if someone gets sick because they weren't told," Mike explained.

"What I need to prove is that Tate Builders knew about it when they built it, or even before they built it, and chose to do nothing about it. Since radon tests are being done more often, and are showing ridiculous levels everywhere, they face a shitload of potential lawsuits."

"You think they're responsible for Susan's death? Are you kidding me?" Ralph yelled. "Tate has built thousands of condo units across the US."

"Well, if not them, maybe their insurance company that stands to dish out millions from these deaths."

"Ralph, I just thought of something you might do to help," Mike said.

"Tate had to have some engineering reports done before they started the condo project. If you can dig into that and try to get me copies of all those reports once you find out what engineering company did the work, there might be something there."

"Maybe if I flash my badge around, I can get this faster than you normally would from the North Smithfield planning department or the land inspector. I'll start on it tomorrow."

CHAPTER 4

In late June, 1989, Samantha Collins was born, a daughter to Bruce and Christine Collins, in Hoboken, New Jersey. Samantha's childhood in the 1990s was like most children as she went from kindergarten to elementary school experiencing what most pre-teen kids go through. Because the Collins' marriage was stable, Samantha's upbringing also was very stable as she experienced both the normal fears and fantasies in her age group.

However, when she turned thirteen, she started having strange recurring dreams. She would scream during the night and, when her mother rushed quickly to her bedroom, Samantha related how she had seen a woman murdered. This dream appeared every several months until she reached the age of sixteen in 2005. She continued to be haunted by her dreams and her parents sought medical advice to see what could be causing this. Samantha attended a dream clinic and began to talk in her sleep about her dreams.

At first, the dreams related to the murder of a woman in a house by a man with a gun. The man was white, wore some type of helmet, and had a scar on his chin and a tattoo of a horse's face on his right forearm. She could not identify this man, or when this supposedly happened. She also had no idea where the murder took place. The doctors indicated to Samantha and her parents she likely had experienced some traumatic episode in her early childhood, whether from watching a television program or from having read about a similar account in a newspaper. They further indicated to Samantha these dreams would likely stop, but exactly when was unknown.

No one but her parents knew about the dreams, and the dreams did not seem to interfere with her social life and school work at the Hudson School, a private school in Hoboken that enrolled less than two hundred students from grade five through twelve. Samantha's parents believed the low teacher-student ratio at Hudson was good preparation for college.

As she reached her senior year at Hudson, Samantha had dated several different boys from Hudson and also from Hoboken High School. None of them made lasting impressions on her, and as she prepared to start looking at possible colleges to attend, the petite teenager with brown hair and eyes hoped to narrow her choice to a few colleges in the Boston area.

In August, 2007, Samantha, an only child, and her parents set up a schedule to visit Boston College, Boston University, and Northeastern University. Samantha leaned toward a teaching career and all of these schools had expressed interest in her once they realized she would likely end at the top of her class coming out of Hudson.

"Why does Boston look familiar to me, Dad? I have never been here before," Samantha asked her father as he drove on Storrow Drive leaving Boston University.

"Could be from some TV show filmed in Boston or somebody you know who has told you a lot about it. Boston gets a lot of publicity, especially with all the pro sports teams here, the marathon, and all the history going back to colonial times. Could be any of those things, Sammy," her father answered.

"No, that's not it, Dad," she said as she told him to take the next left turn while he was driving out of Boston University.

"I know where I am. I can take you from here right to Northeastern, without the GPS or any maps. I can't put my finger on it, Dad. I just know I've been here before."

"You're freaking me out, Sammy, are you serious?"

"Dad, just see if I'm right. We are on Storrow Drive. In less than a mile, there will be an exit for Charlesgate toward Route 1 South and Fenway. Take Fenway off the exit to Hemenway Street. In about a half a mile, you'll be at Huntington Avenue, and that's where Northeastern is," Samantha pleaded with her father to listen to her.

"Okay, okay, but Sammy, if I get lost, the GPS goes right back on," her father said.

During this time, Samantha's mother just sat looking at the sights of Boston, almost to the point of being oblivious to where they were headed. Christine Collins had been educated in upstate New York and did not enjoy big cities, preferring the life in a quiet rural area. But she was not about to discourage her daughter from choosing where she wanted to go to college.

Following a few turns as Samantha had suggested, sure enough, they faced the entrance to the Northeastern campus on Huntington Avenue.

"How did you do that, Sammy?" her father asked.

"I don't know, Dad. It's like I've been here before. I can't explain it," she replied as she shook her head in wonder.

As they parked their car in a visitors' lot near the admissions office, Samantha knew exactly where to go. She never hesitated to get her bearings and instantly headed for that particular building. Her parents hustled to keep up with her.

"This is the place, folks. This is where I want to go."

"But you haven't even seen the place yet. Are you feeling alright?" her mother finally asked. "We haven't even been to Boston College yet in Newton?"

"I can't explain it. There is just something about this place that I like. I know they will offer what I want to study. I know where the dorms are. I don't know how I know these things, but I do."

Before the afternoon was over, Samantha had given her parents an unexpected tour of the entire campus, and her parents were amazed at how this could happen. The admissions office had already reviewed all of her application forms and high school transcript through her junior year, and asked if she wanted to consider early acceptance at Northeastern if it was offered. To her parents' surprise, she said yes. The director of admissions said the school would consider her request and notify her of the next step at some date in the fall.

They never drove to Boston College on that day or on any other day. Samantha was convinced her choice would be Northeastern University, majoring in elementary education.

Her senior year at Hudson was mostly uneventful as she focused on maintaining her high grade point average at the top of her class. Her immediate goal was to be the valedictorian at her graduation in June, 2008. She had received acceptance to Northeastern the previous December and was admitted as an early entrant. In the letter of acceptance from the school, Samantha was informed she qualified for scholarship grants if she achieved the rank of valedictorian, which not only gave her incentive to achieve the goal, but it made her parents happy knowing tuition costs would be much less, if any at all.

The Collins were a middle-income family at best, with Bruce struggling at his flooring sales and installation business and Christine working as a travel planner for a local agency. Neither had a college degree and the thought of their daughter going to college was very satisfying to them. The likelihood of some financial aid in the picture made them even more proud of Samantha than they at first realized.

At the graduation ceremony at Hudson, the principal and headmaster of the school introduced Samantha for her valedictorian address, and she strode to the podium and removed her cap as she approached the microphone.

"Today is the day that we realize how much our parents have learned in the last few years," she began with a smile on her face. "Where we go from here is up to us....or is it?

Fate has a way of disrupting our plans at times, no matter how successful we think we are destined to be. Who knows, some of us may be here today, but gone tomorrow, much sooner than we thought. But who's to say we won't be back again later to try to change what happened the first time?" she continued.

"Imagine being able to relive parts of your life differently than the first time. Imagine for a moment further that you can avoid the same fate in your life the second time around. Imagine also, no one knows you've been here before. It's your little secret, like being able to read someone else's mind without them even knowing you can," she went on.

"Who really knows among us what the future holds? We can only take what we have learned here at Hudson and hope it is enough for us to move forward and make a better life for our own future children than our parents have provided for us. I leave here today with dreams for a better tomorrow, but I'm not even sure I haven't been here before. It is often said you don't get a second chance to make a first impression. But what if you did? What if you could predict your own destiny...in this life, or the next? Who is to say there is no other life after this one? Perhaps, if our paths do not cross again in this life, perhaps they will again on the other side. We live in strange times, and for now, on behalf of the Class of 2008, we bid you farewell until we meet again somewhere out there."

The audience sat there in silence. Then a few claps began, then more, and finally, the applause from her classmates became louder and louder, until everyone in the auditorium rose to their feet and gave Samantha a standing ovation.

Samantha Collins had dared to be different, to speak the unspeakable where life leads to death, which may lead to life again. Only her parents knew what she was talking about, as the demons in her dreams would not go away.

CHAPTER 5

Bonnie Stevens, Mike's legal assistant, had graduated from Bryant College in Smithfield in 1985 and was Mike's first secretary. By 1989, Bonnie had proven to be invaluable to Mike as her keen attention to detail had impressed him more than once. A year earlier, Mike had asked her if she was interested in pursuing paralegal work. Mike had received his quarterly magazine from law school and there was a big ad for the paralegal program there because of the shortage of paralegals in general. He agreed to pay for her tuition and Bonnie jumped at the opportunity. She completed the program in only one year, for what normally took two to three years on a part-time basis.

Bonnie, at age twenty-five, wore a leg brace on her left knee, the result of permanent damage to the knee from a drunken driver who rammed the driver's side of her car after he had sped through a red light. Mike had handled the case and Bonnie collected a hefty settlement from the driver's insurance company. Whether Mike had hired her out of sympathy for her condition, or because he felt confident in her ability to do the job, was something he thought about on occasion. But she had proved to him she was a good asset in the years that followed.

On Monday morning, Bonnie left from the office for her first interview with Peter Clifford, the son of a retired stockbroker who had died the year before in 1988 from lung cancer. Maurice Clifford had retired in 1983 following a very successful career with A.G. Edwards. Success for Maurice, however, had taken its toll. His wife of forty years, Martha, had walked into his office late in the afternoon one day, only to find him in the company of his half-naked secretary. It seems that Maurice had been cheating on his wife for years. Martha suspected his infidelity when she inadvertently caught a whiff of a woman's perfume on one of his dress shirts. The same shirt had a parking garage receipt in the left pocket from the Biltmore Hotel garage in Providence on a day when Maurice supposedly had a brokers' conference in Boston.

Maurice paid dearly for the affairs, and he and Martha had divorced in 1980, leaving her with full custody of their teenage son, Peter. When Maurice died, Peter was named executor of his estate, not that Maurice had much of an estate left after the divorce. Besides the condo, Maurice held a $500,000 life insurance policy with Peter as the beneficiary, and not much else. His company pension and Social Security benefits would cease upon his death.

Following his father's death, Peter immediately had put the condo on the market, and within a few months, sold it.

Peter Clifford, a loan specialist at First Savings & Trust in Rehoboth, Massachusetts, had agreed to talk to Bonnie following her telephone call the week before.

"Hello, I'm here to see Peter Clifford. I have an appointment. My name is Bonnie Stevens," she announced as she entered the bank and walked to a teller station.

"I'm Peter Clifford, Miss Stevens, please come into my office. How may I help you?" he gestured for her to sit down as he faced her across from his desk.

"I'm sorry to bring up the subject of your father's death, Mr. Clifford, but there may be more to his illness than you are aware of. Can you tell me when you started noticing any changes in his health before he died?"

"Well, let's see. He bought the condo in 1980 after he and my mother were divorced. He looked fine to me for several years after that. He was an avid golfer and still played tennis twice a week. So, I didn't see any change in him until about 1985 when he started to cough a lot and kept making raspy sounds, like always clearing his throat. It was annoying to hear it when we got together, because he would do it in a restaurant, on the golf course, everywhere. I told him somebody should look at this and maybe prescribe some kind of medicine to get rid of it. My dad never smoked, so I never ever thought about lung cancer. It just simply never entered my mind," Peter Clifford mentioned.

"A few years before he got sick, he got into train sets and had set up a huge set of tracks with a miniature village all around it, and he loved spending time down there in the basement of his condo. He even added more and more to the arrangement each time I visited, and I bet he spent four to five hours a day down there. I was happy to see him so preoccupied in something, especially in the winter when there was no golf, and tennis was only two nights a week. The train thing seemed to fill up a lot of his time and he loved being down there."

"What happened after the coughing got worse?" Bonnie asked.

"One night, in July, 1987, I believe it was, we were at a restaurant, the Continental Café in Mansfield, when he had one of his coughing spells. When he used his napkin on his lap to muffle the cough, the napkin had blood stains on it. That scared the hell out of me and I insisted he get it checked right away. Within a week, he was diagnosed with advanced stage lung cancer. He had chemo and radiation for months, lost his hair and most of his ability to talk, and died the following spring of 1988. Why do you want to know about my father's death anyway?" Peter asked.

"This may be nothing, Mr. Clifford, but do you remember when you sold his condo after he died?"

"Yes, of course. I told the real estate guy I didn't want it and to please handle the sale for me, which he did."

"Did you know that certain things had to be done to the condo before the real estate agent sold it?" Bonnie asked.

"I knew that the buyers had a home inspection done and the agent handled a few things that needed to be fixed. Why?" Peter inquired.

"Mr. Clifford, have you ever heard of radon gas?"

"No, not really. Should I?"

"Well, the house inspection the buyers wanted before the sale included a radon test. The test uncovered levels of radon gas way above acceptable limits and your agent took care of it by having the gases removed with what is called a mitigation system….a pipe inserted under the condo basement floor and exhausted outside the unit."

"So he took care of the problem, that's what I paid him to do, so what?" asked Peter.

"Mr. Clifford, the level of radon gas in your father's condo was so high, almost five times the acceptable level, that it might have caused your father's lung cancer. High exposure to radon gas can cause lung cancer."

"You're telling me that my father may have caught lung cancer from being exposed to this radon gas in his condo?"

"Not so much from the condo itself as from spending a lot of time in the basement of the condo where the radon gas comes through the floor wherever there are cracks, like in the joints where the floor meets the walls if they are not sealed."

"What exactly are you saying, Miss Stevens? Why are you telling me this?" he asked.

"Your father happens to be one of twelve people who died from lung cancer from this condo complex in the last five years. Do you know what the odds of that happening are other than in a West Virginia coal mine? It is very possible all of these deaths were the result of high levels of radon gas and none of them even knew about it. For years, hardly anyone tested houses for radon gas. You never heard of it yourself, Mr. Clifford."

"But it can be fixed obviously, based on the people who bought my father's unit."

"Yes, but years ago, when the complex was built, someone may have known about the radon level the condos were sitting on. That's what we're concerned about."

"What do you mean?" Peter's voice now reached a higher pitch.

"I mean, if someone, the contractor, the engineers, whoever, if someone knew about the existence of the gas and did not do anything about it, or deliberately chose to ignore it, then maybe somebody here is liable for these twelve people dying, including your father," Bonnie stated firmly.

"If your father's death could have been prevented, Mr. Clifford, if someone deliberately withheld the knowledge of radon gas on the property, wouldn't you want those people to be held accountable for that?"

"Twelve people from Rock Ridge Common all died from lung cancer in the last five years?" he asked surprisingly.

"The number is how many we know about. There could be others who have it, or will get it sooner or later, because no one's told them it might exist. There are over three hundred units at Rock Ridge, many of which have been there since 1980, and the people who own these units have no clue what radon gas is, and what it can do to you. Back then, no one ever tested for radon. There definitely could be others on the verge of getting lung cancer, while many never catch anything because maybe their unit doesn't have any."

"Are you considering a class action suit here, Miss Stevens?" Peter asked.

"We, Michael Strange & Associates, represent a woman whose husband died last year from lung cancer, and she's the one who happened to know of others who died of lung cancer too. None of them smoked, Mr. Clifford, not a single one. If what we find is somebody's willful neglect to inform owners of a potential health hazard on the property, then, yes, we will be prepared to move forward in a class action. But we have a long way to go before that happens. Maybe the other deaths were not related to radon exposure. It is too soon to know at this time, but if we have enough to file such a law suit, would you be willing to be included in it? It would not cost you anything, but if it develops into some kind of settlement from the responsible party, it might be worth it to you?" Bonnie asked.

"Sure, what do I have to lose?" Peter answered.

Bonnie pulled a consent form from her briefcase and asked Peter to read the form before he signed it. Peter scanned the document, signed it, and left his desk for a minute to make a copy of it for his records. Bonnie thanked Peter for his time, asked him not to discuss this with anyone, even other family members, and left his office.

Once back in her car, she glanced at her list and wondered. *Carla Collamati, oh my, she still lives in the condo unit where her husband Bruno died four years ago. I wonder how she is.*

CHAPTER 6

Zeke Goodman was not the brightest bulb on the planet. Zeke was a thirty-five year old three-time loser in the mid-1980s. He had been released on parole from the ACI, Rhode Island's state prison system, short for the Adult Correctional Institution, after he served five years for a conviction of armed robbery at a gas station in Warwick in 1979. By the time the trial ended, and sentencing was pronounced by the presiding judge at his trial, nearly a year had passed.

Once incarcerated at the ACI, he got into a few scrapes early on, but nothing serious enough to affect his parole hearing. And besides, he had kept his nose clean for the entire year before the parole hearing, and had been classified as rehabilitated by the parole board.

Zeke's sister, Helen, had married Jonathan Tate in 1981, while Zeke was still in prison. Helen was thirty-two, three years younger than Zeke, and had a sisterly love for him because he had always protected his little sister when they were growing up in meager housing on the south side of Providence. He would let it be known in the neighborhood that no one messed with his sister or he would see to it they paid the price. Zeke hung around with local street gang members and was always in trouble with the law. Helen and Zeke's parents were Jewish. They had moved to Rhode Island after World War II in 1946 from the Soviet Union and worked long hours in the local mills in Pawtucket, a short jaunt from their small apartment just past the Slater Mill complex. The long hours they spent in the mills meant Zeke was left on his own throughout much of his teenage years, and he surrounded himself with other teens who found it easy to unite to gain attention and the respect they never seemed to get from home.

Helen had asked her husband if he could find work for Zeke with Tate Builders after his pending release on parole. Tate Builders, a house contracting business, had been set up by Jonathan's father in the early 1950s. The contractor had boomed in the 1960s when they erected hundreds of homes in developments in the Pawtucket, Woonsocket, and Cumberland areas of Rhode Island. In the 1980s, however, condominium complexes began to sprout everywhere as an alternative to single family home ownership. For a monthly fee, people would own their own apartments, but without the need to maintain the outside of the property, a very fast-growing concept.

Tate had just purchased several hundred acres of land in North Smithfield, and they were preparing to develop

Rock Ridge Common, a 350-unit condominium complex on the property. The town had arranged for the complex to have town sewage and water through connections with the abutting city of Woonsocket for an annual unit usage fee. Siteco Engineering Company was in charge of laying out the pipework necessary to accommodate such a huge project, which would include a pumping station to handle the water flow from the condos in North Smithfield to Woonsocket's sewer lines.

Jonathan Tate had borrowed over $2 million to purchase the land alone, and another $2 million would be required for soil testing, road construction, and the first phase of unit construction. It was expected that the sale of the first sixty units would then fund further units to be built, as well as repay a portion of the original loan. Jonathan had even used his personal home in Scituate as collateral for the loans. So, hiring Zeke was not a big deal to Jonathan. The gesture would be well-received by his wife, and Jonathan knew Zeke would be indebted to him for the opportunity to get back into the work force. Zeke would be taught how to operate heavy construction equipment, while he assisted Tate's project foreman wherever he was needed.

On his first day at work in June, 1985, Zeke had already had an argument with his new boss, Manny Rodriguez, the fifty-three year old foreman who had been with the company for over thirty years. Jonathan's father had hired Manny in the early 1950s, and Manny had grown into the foreman's rank by making smart decisions for Tate Builders during the housing boom of the 1960s.

Zeke was assigned to unload sheets of plywood outside condo units under construction and to then bring each sheet to the framers who were installing the roofs for these units. The framers were not impressed with the way Zeke worked as he took far too much time, which slowed the roof installations and upset Manny who was determined to stay on schedule in each construction phase. When the framers complained that they always had to wait for the material from Zeke, Manny confronted him to find out what the problem was.

"I'm sorry, Manny, I'm a little new at this physical work, but I'll get better, I promise," he pleaded with Manny.

"Look, Zeke, I know your sister is Jonathan's wife, and I think what he's doing for you is great. But I've got deadlines to meet, and related or not, Zeke, you have to step it up here and keep this work moving."

"Give me a break here, Manny, what's the big deal? It's not as if I've committed a crime here," Zeke replied.

"Do you want this job or not? If I tell Jonathan that you can't handle it, you'll be out of here tomorrow, brother-in-law or not."

Zeke gripped his fists together tightly, but backed away as he tried to keep calm after Manny let him know in no uncertain terms who was in charge. He would someday seek revenge against Manny, even though Manny had merely followed the instructions he had been given himself.

Zeke managed to survive those first weeks at Tate Builders, but quickly realized he was not cut out for this physical work. Jonathan had offered him an opportunity to learn the operation of heavy bulldozers and backhoes, where the brunt of the work is done by the equipment, not the operator. Zeke jumped at this chance and was scheduled to work for the grounds and landscape supervisor, Jerry Tate, Jonathan's brother. Jerry had been a construction equipment operator for twenty years and could handle most equipment he had to. He turned out to be a perfect instructor for Zeke, and they eventually became friends, frequenting the same local bars and sports clubs. Jerry also was single like Zeke, and they both had no other responsibilities after work to attend to. When one of them got into a brawl at a bar following too much to drink, the other would always step in to defend him. Ironically, this tended to keep Zeke out of trouble with the law and with his parole officer, Bob Marcotte.

Marcotte's job was not to try to continue to work on Zeke's rehabilitation, but to see to it he stayed out of trouble and did not violate the terms of his parole. Marcotte thought Zeke Goodman was both rude and obnoxious with people in general, and with him particularly. After a year on parole, Zeke often missed scheduled appointments with Marcotte, but Marcotte let it slide more often than not as the parole duration was about to end. He did not trust Zeke and feared he would somehow be involved in some illegal activity again. He just had a hunch this would happen.

When word reached Marcotte that another parolee had been badly beaten at Jake's Bar & Grille on Main Street in Manville, an informant had told Marcotte that it had been Zeke who had done the dirty work, although the parolee reported it was a stranger he had never met nor seen again since the incident. News of this nature did not ease Marcotte's job, especially when at his following meeting with Zeke shortly after the brawl, Zeke's hands were all bruised and full of scabs, the usual result after a fist fight. Zeke merely replied that the bruises were done when he was repairing a backhoe in a gravel pit on one of the construction sites.

At work, Zeke was now digging trenches for the sewer and water lines in Rock Ridge Common and he worked closely with Siteco Engineering during this phase of the project. While he seemed to handle himself well at this work, Jerry Tate was now free to focus more on backfilling foundations and preparing the grounds for landscaping and the installation of sprinkler systems.

The first phase of the construction moved along on schedule and nearly sixty units were ready for completion. Jonathan was able to use the proceeds from these sales to finance the next sixty unit phase and also to repay $200,000 of the initial loan, which satisfied the bank for now.

Success sometimes brings out a tinge of greed in people. Jonathan and Jerry felt they deserved bonuses for their hard work, and who could fault them. They were the sole owners of Tate Builders. The problem was in the cash they paid themselves. This money was originally intended and earmarked to pay subcontractors doing work on the next phase of the project.

Consequently, Tate Builders started to delay payments to subcontractors, which in turn caused harsh feelings between them, and some went so far as to bring legal action against Tate for money they were owed. A few refused to do any more work until they were paid for previous jobs. Jonathan hoped the sale of the new sixty unit phase would get Tate Builders back on track to pay these workers on time, while also reducing the bank loans further.

Who knew the Tate's upcoming dilemma would test Zeke's loyalty to them?

CHAPTER 7

Ralph Pennington pulled up to the North Smithfield Town Hall on Main Street, in the Slatersville section of town, and walked directly toward the building inspector's office.

"Good morning, I'm Ralph Pennington from the Pawtucket Police Department, and I'd like to get some information on Rock Ridge Common, if I could?" he asked as he flashed his police badge to the clerk at the counter.

"What exactly are you looking for, sir?" the clerk questioned.

"I'm interested in reading up on the engineering report that was presented to the town on that development back in 1980, I believe," Ralph answered.

"Wow, that's a while ago, sir. All the files on Rock Ridge are probably in our file room downstairs."

"That's understandable, ma'am, and is there someone down there who can point me to the files?" Ralph went on.

"You know, Mr. Pennington, I think those files are all on microfiche now. Let me see if I can find those film sheets for you. I can't see anyone going through old file boxes down there. We hardly ever get requests from anyone for stuff like that. What exactly is it you are looking for anyway?" the clerk inquired.

"Well, we have a similar project that is contemplated in Pawtucket, and I'm on a special assignment to take a look at what other large condominium projects in the state went through to get them approved and completed. I guess the city wants to be sure all the environmental issues are covered. Rock Ridge was mentioned because of its size, and I would just like to get a feel for the whole project from engineering, zoning, sewage connections, etc., the whole deal."

"Sounds exciting for Pawtucket. Well, as I recall, the project was done by the Tate Builders and the condos still look great ten years after they've been up. I know quite a few people who live there myself," she replied.

"Good to know the project has done so well." The clerk never for a moment thought to question why a police detective would be seeking this information, as opposed to the city's planning department. To Ralph, this meant his charm at getting information from sources still worked.

A few minutes later, Ralph was escorted to a small room where the microfiche reader was located, with an abutting table allowing users to take notes. The reader had the capability to print pages from the screen, and Ralph was told he would need to insert dimes in the coin slot adjacent to the reader. The clerk indicated she could accommodate him if he needed change, and she left Ralph to his research.

As he began to scan the microfiche files, he came across the name of Siteco Engineering Company of Norwood, Massachusetts and jotted down the name on a pad. He went from frame to frame for several hours. He did not know exactly what he was looking for until he came across a caption entitled "Environmental Concerns." He realized this area was covered by Siteco, but there did not seem to be anything glaring in their report. Wetlands issues seemed to be addressed, EPA issues as well, but no mention any-where about radon. As a matter of fact, the word 'radon' never appeared anywhere.

I wonder if Siteco even was concerned about or tested the grounds for radon, Ralph thought to himself.

Once he was satisfied there was nothing more in the records, he returned the microfiche to the clerk and went on his way.

"Mike, this is Ralph. The only thing in the files in the North Smithfield records on Rock Ridge was the name of the engineering company, Siteco Engineering from Norwood. The records didn't have anything about radon though. Look, it's my day off anyway, so I'm going to take a ride to Norwood and see what I can find," he told Mike from his car phone as he left the town hall. Siteco was about a thirty minute drive on Route 95 North. The company was located on University Avenue in the Norwood Industrial Park, just off the exit from 95.

Ralph had deliberately not called Siteco ahead of time. His police instincts told him not to inform the company of the reason for his visit, just in case the company did have something to hide about Rock Ridge. The element of sur-prise made him feel more comfortable as he strolled through the office doorway and approached the receptionist.

"Good afternoon, may I speak to someone here about the Rock Ridge Common engineering project your firm worked on in North Smithfield in 1979 and 1980?" Ralph asked with a smile on his face.

"Who may I say is calling, please?" the receptionist asked with no expression on her face.

"Detective Ralph Pennington of the Pawtucket, Rhode Island Police Department, calling on behalf of the Town of North Smithfield that needs your help," Ralph answered. He stood there and could not believe how he had just introduced himself.

The receptionist picked up the phone and dialed an extension. She repeated the message exactly to whoever was at the other end of the telephone line.

"Please be seated, Mr. Pennington. Someone will be with you shortly." No sooner than Ralph took a seat in the reception area, a tall, thin, bald-headed man walked down the hallway toward him.

"Mr. Pennington? Hi, I'm Rudy Dionne, one of the engineers on the Rock Ridge Common project about ten years ago. As a matter of fact, I think I'm the only guy left here who worked on the project. John Young, my boss at the time, died a few months ago in a freak accident at his home, and most of the surveyors, soil conservationists and environmental people on the project were subcontractors, and I don't really remember too many of them or where they are today. What exactly are you looking for?"

"Mr. Dionne, I'll be blunt with you. My daughter was murdered a few weeks ago and I don't know why she was killed or who did it. Her husband, my son-in-law, is a lawyer in Providence, and at the time she was killed, he represented a widow whose husband died of cancer, lung cancer to be exact. The guy never smoked, was in great shape, but may have been a victim of too much exposure to radon gas which can cause lung cancer. He lived at Rock Ridge Common and I'm trying to see if there is a connection. I thought one place to start would be to look at the old engineering reports from the preliminary work on the property back then. I know you can just blow me off, Mr. Dionne, but I'll get to see those reports one way or another, even if I have to get a subpoena to do so," Ralph pleaded.

Rudy Dionne looked over at the receptionist's desk and noticed that she was preoccupied with sorting some documents at her desk and did not appear to be listening. He motioned to Ralph to follow him to his office.

"Darlene, hold my calls until I let you know when I'm available. I don't want to be disturbed," he emphasized to her.

"Yes, Mr. Dionne, what about your wife?" she asked.

"No one, Darlene, not unless it's an emergency."

Rudy escorted Ralph down a long corridor lined with drawing rooms, map trays, and an open area where four draftsmen were working on land maps. They reached his office around the next corner of the one-story building. Rudy asked Ralph to sit down in a side chair near his desk as he proceeded to shut the office door, walked to the outside windows and closed the blinds, and walked to the glass window overlooking the open area where the draftsmen were, and pulled the curtain closed. Ralph became a bit edgy at this behavior and wondered what to expect next.

Rudy was forty-five years old, lived in Norwood, and had received his engineering degree from Worcester Polytech in 1966. He had worked at Siteco since graduation. He had started out in the drawing rooms, much the same as the crew he now supervised.

"Ralph, may I call you Ralph?" he asked.

"Sure, that's fine. We are a little more isolated right now than I expected, Mr. Dionne."

"Please call me Rudy. First, let me offer my condolences on the death of your daughter. I have an eighteen-year old myself and I cannot imagine what it would be like if something like this happened to her," he said.

"We are a private company, Ralph. The owner is now semi-retired, and he only comes in to get involved when we are about to sign a new contract, or he wants to meet a new client of ours. He has been plagued with poor vision in the last few years, macular degeneration they call it, and he cannot read plans well at all anymore. But the business has done well over the years, and he can afford to let us handle most of the contract work. He is only fifty-five, Ralph, but spends most of his time at his home in Boca Raton when he is not up here. The owner's name is Rocco Santini. Rocco's wife for the last thirty years is Gloria, formerly Gloria Tate." Ralph's eyes lit up and suddenly he sat up in his chair at the news.

"The only reason we did that job back then was because Rocco was influenced by his wife to do it for her younger brother, Jonathan, who planned the project after he bought all that land in North Smithfield. Rocco back then was pretty particular about the jobs we bid on, and the people we dealt with. A lot of time you're asked to look the other way on EPA issues or wetlands problems, because some local official can get the project approved pretty quickly, but for a price, and usually in cash with no trace to come back to the politicians involved. Jonathan was in way over his head on this thing, but Rocco hoped he would make it work, and he may have let some items slip through the cracks. I'm not sure. I wasn't involved at that level at the time."

"Listen, Rudy, I'm not a rookie here. I've been around the block a few times, and I know about politicians taking bribes. Didn't I just mention to you that I'm from Rhode Island, the capital state of corruption and dirty politicians, from governors to Supreme Court justices, to mayors on down the list? I'm not here to attack your work on the project. I'm here to find out what Tate Builders knew about the North Smithfield site they maybe should have reported to somebody. It sounds to me like somebody didn't want my son-in-law poking his nose into this, and may have tried to scare him off by murdering his wife, my daughter," Ralph said sternly.

"Isn't it a bit drastic, Ralph? I mean, murdering his wife to stop him from digging into a few cut corners on a condo project?"

"Not just a condo project, Rudy, a complex where twelve residents have died of lung cancer in the last five years, and all of them non-smokers. Twelve law suits that, if successful, would cost Tate millions of dollars in settlements to the victims' survivors. Does that sound drastic enough for you now?" Ralph aggressively contended.

Rudy Dionne rose from his chair and walked to the office door. He motioned to Ralph, "I'll be right back, Ralph, just sit back for a few minutes."

Rudy closed the office door behind him as he walked down the hallway toward a corner office. The name on the door read 'Rocco Santini". He pulled out a set of keys and unlocked the door. He looked both ways to be sure no one saw him enter. He closed the door behind him and walked straight for the credenza behind Rocco's desk. He found the file drawer in the credenza locked and again fumbled for a key to unlock it. He then opened the drawer, scanned the file tabs, until he came to the binder report, about two inches thick, that contained the report he was looking for.

He quietly looked out Rocco's office and rushed to a copying machine in an alcove nearby. Rudy fed the copying machine as fast as he could, all the while looking each way to be sure no one saw him. The high-speed copier took about two minutes to get through the entire report. When the job was complete, he took the original report and the copy and returned to Rocco's office to place the original back into the file drawer in the credenza, and he made certain to lock the credenza. He scanned the room to be sure that nothing was out of place as he grabbed the copy and locked Rocco's office door as he left.

When he returned to his office, Ralph was pacing the floor and had a nervous look about him. He seemed wary of Rudy's next move. These were again the instincts of a detective, to be on guard at every moment.

"Please, sit down Ralph; I'm not the enemy here."

Ralph reluctantly took his chair, and all the while never took his eyes off Rudy as he went around his desk to face Ralph. He handed him the copy of the Rock Ridge Common engineering file.

"Ralph, this is our official report to Tate Builders. It covers everything we did there, and our findings. This should also be what Tate gave the town's planning department people back then. If the town's report is not the same as ours, then maybe there is something there you can use. How you got a copy of this report, I'll never tell, but I will deny ever giving you a copy. Are we clear about this?" Rudy emphasized.

"As I said to you earlier, Ralph, I've got a daughter who is likely just a few years younger than your daughter was, and if the Tates have anything to do with this, I hope you get them. I wouldn't put anything past those people. I didn't like them then when I worked on the project, and nothing's changed my mind since then. Put the report in your briefcase. I don't want anyone to see you leave with it. I hope you find who did this."

"I can't believe you're doing this. I mean, you don't even know me. For all you know, I could just be a vengeful father on a crusade to blame anybody for this senseless murder, hoping this firm was as crooked as they get. I think I've been working in Rhode Island too long. Everyone there would be a suspect, and I'd probably find good reason to think this way. You obviously don't think you have anything to hide here," Ralph replied as he rose from his chair.

"Ralph, I've worked for Siteco and Rocco for many years. What I do know is, we don't fudge our work for anyone. Gloria Santini is a wonderful woman, and in her mind, she did the right thing to help out her brother. What he did, or did not do, was up to him. Jonathan Tate is not someone I would trust."

Ralph and Rudy Dionne shook hands and Ralph left his office. As he walked to his car in the company's parking lot, he called Mike from his car phone.

"Mike, I've got the full engineering report from Siteco, and I'll read it tonight after I get home. Isn't this what everyone does on their day off, read a two-hundred page engineering report?" he told Mike.

"Thanks, Ralph. Bonnie had a couple of great visits with two of the victims' relatives today. I'll fill you in on them later. Call me tomorrow when you get out of work."

Ralph loosened his necktie, tossed the briefcase with the report on the passenger seat beside him, and began the drive home to Pawtucket.

CHAPTER 8

Ralph arrived home in Pawtucket at five o'clock, and after he poured himself a small glass of apricot brandy on ice, he began to read the Siteco Engineering report on Rock Ridge Common. His wife, Alice, had not yet accepted the death of Susan at the hands of an unknown assailant. The brutal murder of her daughter and only child left a void in her life, and she had no one other than Ralph to vent her anger to following this terrible tragedy. Alice had refused to be medicated and she had considerable difficulty sleeping at night. At fifty years old, she had looked terrific, enjoyed her teaching career at Brown University more than ever, and had cherished the shopping trips with Susan almost every week until her untimely death. Their relationship was like two sisters rather than a mother-daughter one. Alice looked more like thirty-five than fifty before this brutal incident.

Ralph glanced over to Alice as she prepared dinner, and a tear rolled down his cheek as her drained face now made her look more like she was much older than he had ever seen. She went about dinner without so much as any emotion whatsoever. He put the report aside, rose, and wrapped his arms around her waist from behind and hugged her as tight as he could without squeezing too hard. She stopped what she was doing for a brief moment and grasped his arms around her waist.

"We will find this animal, Alice. I won't stop until we do," Ralph whispered in her ear.

"Oh, Ralph, I never realized how much I would miss her company," she lamented.

"Do you remember we had plans to take the train to New York in August, just the two of us? We were going to see a play, do some shopping, and go to a few nice restaurants on the weekend."

"Just about the time my old Air Force buddies and I were going fishing in New Hampshire. Yes, I remember the two of you counting the days after you both were done teaching for the summer. No one can take those memories away, not even the person who did this to Susan. As bad as we feel, put yourself in Mike's shoes. Your wife is murdered because of a case you're working on. How bad do you think he feels? He needs my help on this, and I've got to be there for him. I don't think he's slept in almost a week now. He looks exhausted, and I don't know how he can even stay awake much longer. But he's determined to see this through."

"I know, Hon. I wish I could help somehow, but I know that his dad has a lot of time since his retirement from Texon, and works on the law suit with Mike. Since Linda died two years ago from cancer, Carl Strange's retirement plans sort of went out the window. I remember Mike telling us how he was worried about his father living alone in their big house in Lincoln," Alice added. "I guess we can now say the same about Mike living in a big house in Cumberland all by himself. Why is this happening to us, Ralph?"

"I'll find out, honey. Susan will always be with us, even though we don't see her. She's with us, Alice, I know she's here."

Ralph released his hold on Alice's waist and walked back to his chair in the living room. He sipped his brandy and opened the report.

The first fifty pages were the same as what Ralph had seen from the microfiche at the North Smithfield Town Hall earlier that day. Suddenly, on page fifty-one, there appeared the title "Environmental and Hazardous Material." The section read:

The property rests on two-hundred acres of farmland, south of Main Street, in the Slatersville section of the Town of North Smithfield, and was the subject of a U.S. Geological Survey because of its vast size and end purpose as residential properties. The survey included the determination of the content of radium in the soil and underlying rocks, as well as the permeability and moisture content of the soils. The geologic map provided by the U.S. Geologic Service showed the type of rocks and geologic structures in this specific area. This map further identified the general level of uranium and radium present in the rocks and soil. In this area, the survey showed a high level of uranium present, not uncommon in many regions of New England.

This uranium deposit in the project's soil composition prompted Siteco Engineering to measure the level of radon gases in the soil air. The radon concentration is determined by testing the decay of the radon in the air. Siteco buried a charcoal canister in the soil at varied locations throughout the site, and at multiple intervals to assure consistency in the test results.

Ralph could not read fast enough as he continued......

Our findings were that the levels of potential radon infusion in the soil in question warrant further corrective action by the developer to prevent a potential health hazard to eventual property owners. The readings of soil radioactivity clearly indicate an abnormal preponderance of radon gases below the surface, likely due to the rock formation below such surface.

The geology and soil of the area show an increased likelihood of the presence of elevated levels of radon. The uranium-rich rocks in the area, the highly permeable soils present, and the apparent fracture of underlying rocks with pockets of limestone caverns, all contribute to these findings.

It is our conclusion that the condominium units to be constructed be sealed at the floor and walls of the base foundation in each unit to mitigate any infiltration of radon gas into the units. Without such precautionary measures, the emanation of radon gases would create a long-term health hazard to residents of the units.

Ralph jumped up from his chair and shouted.

"Son of a bitch, son of a bitch. Tate Builders knew there was radon under the ground. They didn't want to spend the money to fix it, so they ignored it and didn't tell anybody. Do you believe this?" he motioned to Alice.

"Are you sure, Ralph? You had better call Mike. I'll hold supper up for a few minutes," she answered.

Before he called, Ralph looked at the photocopies from the microfiche he had taken at the town hall. In the section labeled "Environmental and Hazardous Material", there was merely a one-paragraph summary which indicated none were present. The copy read:

Siteco Engineering's review of soil and rock structures on the property were done and utilized data from the U.S. Geological Survey, and did not reveal any unusual soil characteristics detrimental to the use for residential purposes. There does not appear to be any hazardous materials present in the soil or on the site in question.

Ralph picked up his portable phone and hit the speed dial for Mike's office. Ralph wasn't certain if Mike would still be there at six o'clock, but he was fully aware of the long hours attorneys spent at their offices. The odds were in his favor when Mike answered.

"Mike Strange, how may I help you?"

"Mike, the bastards knew about radon on the property. Way back in 1979, Siteco did all kinds of tests on the property," Ralph said excitedly.

"Ralph, are you sure about this? Is that what it says in their report?" Mike inquired.

"Tate changed Siteco's report when it gave it to the town planning department. I've got what Siteco gave Tate and it's full of stuff about high levels of radon. Siteco even has a section where they recommend that Tate seal all the floors and wall connections in all the units to eliminate the hazard."

"Ralph, do not discuss this with anyone, you understand? If you told Alice, tell her not to mention this to anyone either. No one, Ralph. Put the Siteco report in an envelope or a folder and hide it until I get over there. Don't answer the doorbell unless it's me, are you clear on that?" Mike emphasized.

Mike slammed the receiver down, rose from his chair as he grabbed his suit coat, and stormed out the office after he made certain he locked the door behind him. He took the elevator down to the parking garage below and drove straight for Pawtucket. Within twenty minutes, Mike rang Ralph's doorbell. Excitedly, as he entered, he could not get his hands on the Siteco report fast enough. As he scanned the environmental section and compared it with what was filed at town hall, he realized Tate Builders had excluded the entire comments and recommendations about radon gas.

There was still much more to do, but Mike's firm would start to prepare the law suit against Tate Builders and Mutual of New England. Before the suit would be filed, he needed Bonnie to complete her visits to the rest of the victims' families to determine the scope of the law suit and the potential damages to be covered. Bonnie had seven more visits to make.

CHAPTER 9

Mike had trouble containing his enthusiasm at the information his father-in-law had uncovered. He arrived at his office early the next morning, still all-fired up at the thought of his next moves.

When Bonnie arrived shortly before nine o'clock, Mike called her into his office to find out what her schedule for the day looked like.

"Well, Mike, I was going to try to do three or four more interviews at the condo complex and, hopefully, get them all to sign on to the case like the ones I already have. Why, did you have something else in mind?" she asked.

"No, quite the contrary, Bonnie. I need for you to complete those interviews in the next two days, if you can?" Mike answered.

"Wow, someone's in a hurry. What is it I don't know about here, boss?"

"The Tates knew about the radon back in 1979 and, according to everything we have, they did nothing about it. As a matter of fact, it looks like they gave the town a doctored report, conveniently excluding any mention of radon. So, once you get the rest of these people on board, I think we're ready to file. Just remember not to mention anything about the environmental report to the condo owners, not yet."

"I'll try to get them done by tonight if I can reach all of the ones that are left to do. It might be real late, but I'll do my best, Mike."

With the goal for the day quite ambitious, Bonnie jumped into her Toyota Corolla and left Providence on Route 146 North to North Smithfield. The six remaining surviving spouses all still lived in the units where their spouses had died over the last few years. The surviving spouses ranged in age from fifty-two to seventy.

One after another, Bonnie explained the situation in the complex and the possibility of wrongful deaths due to negligence by the contractor. In four of the six interviews, the survivors had never even heard of radon. But although Bonnie had asked these people not to discuss the issue with anyone, she knew all too well the more people who knew, the more likely the news would reach the Tates. There were still some Tate supporters in condo units, and Bonnie did not rule out some confrontation before her last interview was done.

At noon, she left her third completed visit and was quite pleased at her progress as she walked to her car in the visitors' spaces near the condo owners designated spots. When she eyed her car, she noticed the four flat tires and two large scratches across each side of her door panels. She picked up her car phone and called Mike.

"Well, guess what? The Tates know we're here, Mike. I've got four flat tires and wicked scratches all over my car."

"Call the police and file a report with them once they get there. We need to show a record of all this if we have to. Do you have your Polaroid camera with you?

"Yes, I do. It's in the trunk."

"Make sure you take pictures of the car before you call a service garage. Whatever your insurance doesn't cover for the repairs, I'll take care of. But, watch yourself, Bonnie. Who knows what they're planning next. As a matter of fact, I'm coming over right now. Have you had lunch yet?"

"No, I've got my lunch in the car."

"First, call the police. Next, while you're waiting for them to arrive, grab your lunch and we'll grab a bite together when I get there. I can be there in about a half hour."

Mike was worried. If the Tates were responsible for Susan's murder, Bonnie's life would probably be in danger the more snooping around she did. Bonnie was no fool, and would likely realize what was happening. The faster Mike could get to the condos, the more reassured he would be of her safety. He thought about the danger she was in, and felt responsible that he put her in this position, even though he never expected anything to happen this quickly. He called Ralph to let him know of the incident, but Ralph was not surprised. He thought the local police would handle the issue properly.

Mike arrived at Rock Ridge at twelve-forty-five and found Bonnie standing on the curb near her car. She motioned to the policeman that she saw no one near her car, and he jotted down all the information he needed to file his report. Bonnie had called her insurance company and the agent had instructed her to get a body shop to tow the vehicle and an agent would determine the repair costs after a discussion with them.

"You okay?" Mike yelled as he approached her, giving her a much-needed hug to try to calm her down.

"Yea, I'm fine, a little pissed off, but fine."

"How about the two of us, after lunch, cover the rest of these interviews together?"

"Is this my big brother protecting me here?" she asked with a smile.

"No one's ever called me that, but let's say I've already lost one too many people I care about," he answered boldly as he held Bonnie by both arms. She blushed as he released her from his arm grip and escorted her to his car nearby.

Once the police cruiser with the two police officers left the parking lot, Mike and Bonnie waited for the tow truck to arrive. Mike had stopped at a nearby McDonald's, and the two of them ate lunch in dead silence. They were able to finish lunch before the truck finally arrived. Once the vehicle was hoisted to the back of the truck, Bonnie and Mike drove to the next condo unit using Mike's car. The unit was several blocks further from where they were, and each condo section had its own visitors' parking spaces.

As soon as the last interview was over, Bonnie pulled out the folder that contained all but one of the twelve approval forms from the victims' families. She handed Mike the eleven agreements as she breathed a sigh of relief.

"I'll get a rental for tomorrow morning and pick up the lone approval form that's left. That would be Mrs. Steele in 601. She wanted her son to review the form first, and asked me to come back tomorrow."

"That's great, Bonnie, terrific job."

Mike drove her to the Hertz rental office behind the Biltmore Hotel in Providence and left her there as she gave him the sign that she had a vehicle rented. Mike went back to the office to see if he had any messages on his answering machine. Bonnie was exhausted and drove home in her rented vehicle.

She had made arrangements with Mrs. Steele, the only remaining claimant to sign on to the law suit, to stop by at nine o'clock the following morning. For now, she kicked off her shoes as she entered her apartment, popped a TV dinner in the microwave, and poured herself a glass of chardonnay.

The next morning, she drove directly from her apartment in the Kirkbrae section of Lincoln to Route 146 and exited on the Forestdale ramp toward the condo unit not far from the center of Slatersville Village. She passed the town hall and suddenly her car was rammed from behind by a blue pickup truck. The jolt shook her up and the truck whacked the back side of her car again. The force of the second impact caused her car to go out of control and she could see her car headed directly toward a grove of trees off the road. The rental slammed into a tree and Bonnie's body lunged forward toward the windshield. Her head slammed against the glass and she passed out, her head covered with cuts and broken glass. The pickup truck sped away as quickly as it had appeared.

When Mike received a call from one of the same police officers who had been at the scene of vandalism the day before, he was surprised.

"Mike Strange, how may I help you?"

"Mr. Strange, this is Officer Mulcahey from the North Smithfield Police Department. We met yesterday at Rock Ridge."

"Oh, sure, what can I do for you, Officer?"

"There's been an accident here in Slatersville. I'm afraid it's Miss Stevens, your assistant. Her vehicle rammed a tree head-on and she was seriously hurt, sir. They rushed her to Landmark Medical Center. I thought you would want to know."

"Shit, this is no accident, Officer Mulcahey, not two days in a row. Is she still alive?"

"All I know is she had a head injury and was unconscious when the ambulance left. We're trying to find anyone who may have witnessed what happened, but nothing so far, although it does look suspicious."

"Why do you say that, Officer?"

"Because the rear bumper of the car and the dents near the trunk indicate a blunt force to the rear of the car, not normal for a car ramming into a tree."

"Keep me posted, please. Somebody has to have seen something."

Mike again sped to the hospital as quickly as he could. When he arrived at the emergency room, an area he knew far too well, he asked the attendant where Bonnie Stevens was taken.

CHAPTER 10

"Miss Stevens is in a coma, Mr. Strange. She had a severe blow to the head when she hit the windshield, causing internal bleeding in the brain. We managed to stop the bleeding, and gave her several pints of blood, but we won't know the extent of her head trauma for some time. We have a monitor on her around the clock," Dr. Tardif told Mike.

As Mike entered the ICU, Dr. Tardif told him he could stay there for as long as he wanted. Bonnie had no relatives that Mike was aware of. She lived alone in Kirkbrae Apartments in Lincoln, and as far as Mike knew, she did not have a boyfriend or even other women friends she hung around with. She had always been conscious of her disability since her accident, and kept to herself when she was not at the law office.

Her entire skull was covered in bandages, her left arm in a sling, and cuts and bruises covered most of her face. Her lips were swollen and her face was nearly unrecognizable. It took all of Mike's strength to just look at her. The monitor readings were stable, according to Dr. Tardif, but the slightest change would trigger immediate attention by the staff. Dr. Tardif asked Mike for his car phone number and his office number in the event he needed to reach him quickly on her life-threatening condition, especially if it required her to be transferred to Rhode Island Hospital's neurosurgery ward.

Mike was now furious. You could easily see the hatred in his face. He left the hospital and drove straight to his Providence office. Within a few hours, he had completed the necessary papers to file suit against Tate Builders and Mutual of New England for willful neglect to report a potential hazardous condition at Rock Ridge Common, death resulting. The suit was filed on behalf of twelve plaintiffs, all claiming a wrongful death as a result of withholding information from buyers of condominium units.

Mike knew the murder of his wife and the deliberate attempt on Bonnie were related, a message to him to back off in a case which involved Rock Ridge Commons. The challenge now was to prove it. He would have his day in court. The case now became one of revenge to Mike, as much as justice for the victims' families.

There were no leads on Susan's killer and the Cumberland police were frustrated when no witnesses saw any activity at the Strange's house on the day of the murder. Although the police determined the gunman likely posed as a Venture Cable repairman, no one saw the person, just the Venture truck in front of the house. Venture had reported one of their vehicles stolen from the repair lot on Route 146 in Lincoln the night before. The truck was recovered two days later, a short distance from the repair lot but, once the lab specialists checked the vehicle for prints or any clues left behind, they found nothing.

Although Ralph, Susan's father, often spoke with the sergeant in charge of the case in Cumberland, he knew of many such cases which remained unsolved for quite some time. Ralph had personally been involved in several cold cases in Pawtucket, but homicides were not his specialty on the Pawtucket police force.

* * *

Zeke Goodman thought his brother-in-law, Jonathan, would be greatly indebted to him for all he did to prevent further investigation on the radon issue. He had overheard Jonathan and Jerry Tate talk about an attorney who repre- sented some condo owners whose spouses had died of lung cancer in the last few years at Rock Ridge. Although they had expressed genuine concern on the impact such a law suit would have on future projects once the law suit became public, the Tate brothers were not criminals in their own mind, merely building contractors who cut a few corners at Rock Ridge to save money.

Zeke acted alone in the murder of Susan Strange, and also acted alone in rear-ending Bonnie Stevens off the road in Slatersville. Jonathan Tate was no fool. Perhaps he was greedy, and had very little scruples in his approach to get projects completed under budget, but the attractive visible appearance at all his projects caused units to sell quickly. He soon found the success at Rock Ridge not only paid off his loans to the bank, but enabled him and his brother to pocket millions of dollars of profit in the process.

The coincidence of Susan Strange's death, coupled with the Bonnie Stevens' incident, was worrisome to Jonathan. He found these to be more than a coincidence when an attorney, whom he never met, was the target because he was the orchestrator of a class action suit against him. It wouldn't take a genius to link the two incidents together.

"You didn't do anything stupid, did you Zeke?" Jonathan asked him one day at a local bar shortly after the newspaper account about Bonnie Stevens was published.

"Johnny, don't worry, none of this stuff will ever get to you or Jerry. Besides, the less you know, the better it is for you guys," Zeke replied with a smirk on his face.

"You stupid fool; do you know what you've done?"

"I just may have saved your sorry asses. That's what I did. I told you, don't lose any sleep over this. I've covered my tracks and nobody's ever going to know anything."

"I never told you to do anything on this. It's none of your business. You just work here because you're my wife's brother. Shit man, you've got a record, and we've got a law suit against us. What makes you think this guy Strange doesn't connect you to this somehow?"

"He can do what he wants, Johnny, but he can't prove a thing. I told you I've got it covered. Don't worry about it."

"You might be my wife's brother, you jackass, but if I ever hear about you doing anything other than your construction job ever again, brother-in-law or not, I'll turn you in myself. Do you hear me?"

"Jesus, Johnny, I thought you guys would be grateful that I took care of this for you," Zeke replied.

"Do you know what you've done? You killed the guy's wife and you ran his legal assistant off the road. I'd be so pissed off at you that I'd probably go after you myself, if I was him. I just hope he doesn't think we had anything to do with it, but I doubt it. You may just have pissed off the wrong guy, you jerk."

"Then I can take care of him too, Johnny."

"What the hell is between those ears, Zeke? Don't you hear me? Stay away from anything about this case. Just do your job and keep your mouth shut."

CHAPTER 11

Samantha Collins spent her junior year at Northeastern uneventfully. In May, 2011, following her final exams, Samantha had decided to accept a teaching assistant's position there for the summer months. Northeastern held summer graduate classes for teachers and she had been asked by her elementary school education counselor if she had any interest. She would be allowed to stay rent-free in her private dorm room until the fall semester and the money she could earn would help pay for room and board in her senior year. The graduate program was for only six weeks and would end in the second week of August. Samantha told her parents she would still have half of May and half of August to be home with them in Hoboken.

At first, her parents weren't happy she would stay in Boston for most of the summer, but at age twenty-one,

Samantha was a very responsible person. And besides, there was Alex. Alex Brien was in the same year as Samantha and lived in nearby Arlington. They had both been in an education course together, and just happened to sit next to each other on the first day of class. One thing led to another, and before you knew it, they became nearly inseparable. Alex's parents owned a French restaurant in Somerville, La Mâison Henri, and Alex and Samantha dined there often. His parents simply adored Samantha and believed one day the two would be married.

Samantha had never told Alex about her nightmares, nor did she intend to. She was still convinced in her mind the dreams would eventually go away. But quite the reverse occurred. The dreams became more frequent and started to include visions of another man and different locations, not just of the murder scene. Alex became the distraction she needed and their relationship began to blossom into love. Samantha felt secure around Alex, a muscular six-footer with rich dark hair and eyes. Yet, he was very gentle and polite around her despite his rugged features, perhaps a result of the courtesy that was always extended in a restaurant atmosphere. Hospitality was in his veins and Samantha thought he would make a fine teacher one day. He was a good listener and an even better role model for others to emulate.

While they had sex more than once in her dorm room during their junior year, Alex had never stayed throughout the night. Samantha still did not want anyone to witness one of her nightmares once she fell asleep. She realized she would one day have to confide in Alex about these recurring episodes, but only when the time was right.

Samantha's parents had met Alex at the parents' week-end the previous fall, and had eaten at La M ison Henri where they met his parents, Marcel and Jeanne Brien.

While Alex spent the bulk of his summer vacation working as a maître 'd at the restaurant, Samantha would spend up to six hours a day, three days a week, in the teacher assistant position. She would work from nine o'clock in the morning to noon, and again from six o'clock to nine in the evening on Monday, Tuesday, and Thursday. The afternoons were too warm at this time of year to hold classes since the classrooms were not air-conditioned. Alex planned his schedule to also be off on Wednesday when the two would spend the day together. Sometimes they would go to the beach in Revere, or to a ballgame in Boston. Weekends were difficult for Alex to be off when the restaurant was at its busiest. But like most fine restaurants in the summer, dining hardly ever began before six o'clock at night. So, Alex and Samantha would spend the afternoons together nearly every day.

"Sammy, look here. Josh Groban is appearing in Providence at the Providence Performing Arts Center on a Wednesday in early August. Are you interested? We could spend the day in Providence, maybe visit the Roger Williams Park zoo, have an early dinner at Hemenway's right on the water, then take in the show. The show would probably end around nine-thirty or so, and we could drive back to Boston and be home before eleven," Alex asked as he read the Sunday edition of the Boston Globe.

"If they still have tickets, that sounds like a great idea, Alex."

"Well, I assume they still have tickets if I'm reading this in this morning's paper, Sammy," he answered with a smug look about him.

"I know that, wise guy. I mean if they have good seats left. I don't want to sit at the back of the theater for a concert," she replied with a smirk on her face.

"I'll go online tomorrow and check it out."

Wednesday, August 17, 2011, the day of the concert, arrived quickly as Alex and Samantha had spent so much time together they actually talked seriously about their plans for the future after graduation in May, 2012. While there had been no talk of marriage yet, they both seemed ready to make the inevitable leap.

Alex picked her up at her dorm at ten o'clock and they began the ninety-minute drive to Providence in his 2006 Mazda Miata MX-5 convertible. It was already ninety degrees in Boston and the breeze from the open top car would be welcome as they approached Route 95 South in Stoughton.

"Alex, do you believe people may have lived before in a previous life?" Samantha asked.

"Oh, I've never given it much thought. But do you mean like the old movie *The Reincarnation of Peter Proud* where this guy has dreams he lived before and was murdered?" he answered.

"Yes, something like that."

"Why do you ask?" he inquired.

"I've never told this before, but when I was about thirteen, I started having recurring dreams of seeing a woman murdered. I still have this dream once in a while, but now other people are in the dreams, people I don't know and places I don't ever remember going to. It scares me sometimes, Alex, because the dreams don't go away."

"Have you talked to anyone about this?"

"Oh, sure. My parents took me to some doctor who specializes in dream disorders, and he thought the dreams would go away at some point, but they haven't. And it's been over seven years now," she went on.

"When my parents drove up with me to look at schools in Boston, I was able to guide my father from B.U. right to Northeastern without a map or GPS system, and I had never been to Boston before. Then one night I dreamt I saw a wedding on a beach in Maui. The man was tall and good looking, and the woman was the same one I still see in my dreams who gets murdered. Am I talking weird right now? Am I some kind of loony tunes here?"

"Well, if you are, you sure hide it well. There has to be some explanation for this, and obviously no one's been able to find one yet. And maybe there's more to this than you know."

The conversation continued between the two until they were confronted with a flashing road sign that described an accident ahead. The sign recommended motorists driving to Providence to exit to Route 295 South to Route 146 South to reach Providence to avoid unnecessary delays.

Alex took the exit ramp recommended and began the five-mile drive on Route 295 to Route 146. As they drove toward Exit 11 on Route 295, there was a sign advertising Phantom Farms before the exit.

"Alex, do me a favor. Take this exit. I know this place."

"Have you ever been here before? I thought you told me you've never been to Rhode Island, even after three years in Boston."

"I've never set foot in this state in my life, Alex, but I know this place. Humor me. Let's see what happens."

At the end of the ramp, Samantha told Alex to turn right. A half mile later, they approached an old wooden building with a gravel parking lot and he stopped the car as he pulled in facing the Phantom Farm sign atop the building.

"I know this area," Samantha shouted.

"Are you sure you've never been here before?"

"Never," Samantha replied as she gazed at the building.

Alex began to leave the parking lot to return to the entrance to Route 295. Once he began to take a curve in the road, Samantha told him to take the next right turn, Burke Road.

"171 Burke Road. Stop the car, Alex, please stop the car," she yelled.

She ran up the driveway and rang the front doorbell, Alex racing behind her to catch up.

"Sammy, what are you doing?" he asked furiously.

A young woman in her late thirties answered the door holding a small child in her arms.

"Excuse me, but are you the original owner of this house? It looks very familiar to me. I know this sounds crazy, ma'am, but I seem to know this house."

"My husband and I have lived here since June, 2000. We bought it from an attorney who had done some legal work for us and wanted to sell the place. He lived here alone and the house had bad memories for him, so he moved to Berkshire Estates off Bear Hill Road. He also has a home in Hawaii. He was a nice man, and a good lawyer, but he always looked sad. His wife was murdered back in 1989, and they never caught the person responsible for her death."

"You have three bedrooms. The master is in the back with a separate soaking tub and shower, and a back deck. In the basement, there are French drains all around the perimeter of the floor. Outside your bedroom window, there is an eight-foot pipe in the ground, buried there because there was water coming in the basement and the contractor had inserted the pipe to pump out the water. The pipe was capped a year later and the area was reseeded."

"You're right about the bedrooms, but I'm afraid I don't have a clue about all the basement stuff. I hardly go down there."

"In this front corner, under the picture window outside, there is a St. Joseph statue, buried there for luck."

"I'm afraid I can't help you there either."

"Can you at least tell me the previous owner's name?" Samantha asked.

"Sure, Mike Strange. He has an office in Providence."

"Do Gordie and Betty Landry still live across the street?" Samantha asked as she pointed to the house directly across.

"Yes, they do. Their two sons are just about your age, early twenties," the woman answered.

"They should be around forty-five or so by now. Does Gordie still do mortgage work?"

"As far as I know. Why, do you know him?"

"Not directly, but I used to live around here some years ago and someone pointed out their house to me back then," Samantha answered as she thanked the young woman for the information, and she and Alex left.

Alex looked at her in a frightened way as they rushed away from the doorway down the steps from the farmer's porch and back to the car. He started the car and, as soon as Samantha had shut her door, sped away down the road. About five hundred yards down the road, he pulled off to the side and yelled.

"What the hell was that all about? What's going on here, Sammy? You are freaking me out right about now.

How do you know all this stuff? Are you some kind of a seer or a medium who talks to the dead? Talk to me."

"When I was younger, Alex, I used to get this dream, I told you, over and over again, about a woman getting murdered in her home by a guy with a scar on his chin and a tattoo of a horse's face on his left arm. All I could remember was his face and the construction helmet he wore. I can still see his face in my dreams once in a while. Doctors back then thought I might have had nightmares from some TV show or newspaper article. They told me it would go away as I got older, but it hasn't. I seem to remember more and more about the woman who was killed every time I think about her," Samantha blurted. She turned to Alex, and looked at him very seriously.

"Alex, this is where she lived, I'm sure of it. You heard me, I could describe that woman's entire house and I never set foot inside, and the woman never denied it. How did I know the names of the neighbors across the street?" she went on.

"It's scary to me too, Alex, I can't explain it, but I think I was this woman in another life. I know this sounds crazy, but how can you explain it?"

"I don't know what to say, Sammy. I just don't know what you are going through right now."

CHAPTER 12

It was only three o'clock when they got back on Route 295 in the direction of Route 146 South to Providence. The ride was done in dead silence as Alex still shook his head in wonder at what just happened, while Samantha sat there speechless. They entered the city from an exit ramp on Atwells Avenue, took a left turn toward the downtown area as Alex's GPS system guided him toward the Performing Arts Center. Alex found a parking lot about two blocks from the theater on Dorrance Street. Still silent, they began to walk toward the theater when Samantha stopped dead in her tracks and faced an office building. As if in a trance, she headed through the revolving door and walked to the directory on the wall in the lobby. Alex turned to see where she had gone, and followed her into the building.

"Look, Alex, third floor, room 304, Law Office of Michael Strange and Associates. I know him, Alex, I think he was my husband," she spoke as she turned to him.

"What do you mean your husband? You've never been married," Alex answered.

Samantha walked to the elevator door which was open, got in and pressed three on the elevator control board. Alex followed but did not know why he followed.

The receptionist inside Room 304 greeted them with a broad smile.

"Hi, welcome to the Law Office of Michael Strange & Associates. How may I help you?" she asked.

"I'm here to see Michael Strange, please, I don't have an appointment."

"Mr. Strange is not in the office at this time. Can someone else be of some help?" the receptionist asked.

"No, I need to speak directly with Mr. Strange only. Can you tell me how I can reach him?" Samantha went on.

"Well, that would be pretty difficult right now. He doesn't practice full-time any longer, and most of the firm's cases are handled by other attorneys in the firm. What is this about?"

"It's a personal matter. Does he still live in Berkshire Estates, off Bear Hill Road in Cumberland?"

"He's not in town, ma'am. He has a place in Hawaii and spends a lot of time there. We don't see him except around the holidays. He usually has conference calls with most of the lawyers. That's about as much involvement as he has these days. I'm sorry I can't be of more help to you."

"Thank you very much. You have been more helpful than you can imagine," Samantha replied. They left the law office and she grabbed one of the firm's brochures on the way out.

As they walked to the elevator and stood there, Samantha flipped through the brochure and pointed to a group photo of the firm's lawyers.

"That's Mike Strange, Alex. We were married in 1988, one year before I was murdered in the house we just came from. We went to Northeastern together before this happened and met on the commuter train to Boston. Now I know why I knew so much about Northeastern even before I enrolled. Am I going crazy, Alex? Why is this happening to me?" she pleaded.

"Sammy, there's got to be a reasonable explanation for all of this. I just don't know what it is," Alex responded scratching his head as they entered the elevator.

"Look, we've got plenty of time before the concert. It's only three-thirty. We passed the library on Dorrance Street, just a short walk from here. Would you come with me for just one more stop? I promise this will be it for today, and we can figure this out another day. Even I'm getting confused by all of this," she added.

"What's at the library anyway?" Alex asked.

"I want to check the newspapers for June, 1989 to see if what I believe happened back then, really did happen. I promise, no more than a half hour at most."

"Wow, as weird as this sounds, you've even got me interested in what's going on here."

They walked briskly down Dorrance Street to the main entrance of the Providence Public Library and, after referring to the directory in the lobby, hurried to the reference desk on the second floor. Samantha told the clerk they were from Boston, but doing research on a murder of a woman that occurred in Cumberland in June, 1989. The clerk promptly led them to a section devoted to past issues of the Providence Journal which were kept on library computer terminals. The newspapers were categorized by year, then by month, down to each day of the month. The clerk excused herself, but offered her assistance if they had difficulty finding the information they searched for.

Samantha sat down at the terminal and quickly went to 1989 with the cursor and clicked on the month of June. She then quickly scanned each day's news, which seemed to take forever. After nearly a half hour, she was ready to give up and leave, until Alex told her to at least finish the month.

He grabbed a chair next to her and took charge of the keyboard. Nothing showed up through June 28. When he continued to Thursday, June 29, 1989, the front page headline read *Homosexual Prostitution Inquiry in D.C. shakes up White House.* No other story on the front page caught his attention. But on page three of the Journal, his eyes fixated on the headline.

Wife of Providence Lawyer Murdered in Cumberland

CUMBERLAND: Susan Strange, 27, wife of Providence attorney, Michael Strange, was found murdered yesterday from multiple gunshot wounds, the apparent result of a house break-in gone wrong. A neighbor, Gordon Landry, found Mrs. Strange unconscious on her living room floor and immediately called for rescue personnel using 911. He had gone there to see if everything was okay when her husband could not reach her on their house telephone. Living room furniture was in disarray leading the Cumberland Police Department to believe there was a struggle before the shooting. Police Chief Ed Harrington indicated the case was in its early stages, and there were no witnesses who came forward with any information, nor were there any suspects at this time. Mrs. Strange, an elementary school teacher, was the daughter of Sgt. Ralph Pennington of the Pawtucket Police Department and his wife, Alice.

Alex proceeded to print a copy of this article and the two left in silence. As they walked back toward Westminster Street on Dorrance Street, Alex spoke first.

"I've never thought about this reincarnation stuff. So, I guess I never believed it was possible. There is no way you would know this information I'm holding in my coat pocket unless you were there. Are you sure you want to go to this concert? I'm just dumbfounded by all this, and I don't know what to say."

"So, you don't think I'm crazy by knowing all this?" she asked.

"You're not crazy, maybe a little weird to me right now, but not crazy," Alex answered.

"I need your help to figure this out, Alex. I'm afraid to look into this any deeper. I don't know who else I can talk to, but I'm starting to remember more and more each day. I don't even know if they've ever caught this guy."

"I'm not going anywhere, except maybe for a bite to eat. This is more than I expected today, and I'm hungry. I still like Hemenway's down the street for an early dinner. After a nice glass of wine and some dinner, we can decide if Josh Groban still interests you. By the way," Alex smiled, "what am I having for dinner?"

She poked him hard on the shoulder as they finally smiled to each other and entered the restaurant.

Josh Groban would never sound as good as tonight, she thought.

CHAPTER 13

Bonnie's parents were both deceased, ironically from a head-on crash in 1985 with a drunk driver. Bonnie and her sister, Kathy, were the sole heirs to the parents' estate. Since the sisters did not want to keep the parents' house, they split the proceeds when the house was sold in early 1986.

Bonnie's share of the estate after the sale of the house came to nearly $300,000. She had asked Mike for advice on a safe investment for most of her inheritance, and a financial advisor that Mike was friendly with recommended a conservative balanced mutual fund as the logical choice. She kept her financial status very private and, except for Mike and her sister, no one else knew how well off she was at the young age of twenty-five.

Mike had convinced the North Smithfield police of the imminent threat on her life if news was announced that she was still alive. He insisted that a police officer be placed on duty outside her hospital room twenty-four hours a day for the time being. Police Chief Vinny Plasse agreed to post a security guard immediately.

The crime lab had been able to detect blue paint chips from the rear bumper of Bonnie's rental car after the accident. Two patrons, having breakfast at Terry's Diner on Main street in Slatersville, told the police they had seen a blue pickup truck speed away from the accident scene from their window table at the diner that morning. They were too busy running toward the Maxima slammed against a tree to notice the license plate or the driver of the truck.

The day after the assault on Bonnie, Zeke Goodman pulled into Frank's Body Shop and Auto Sales in Bellingham, Massachusetts. Zeke had purchased the used 1987 Chevy pickup from Frank Mohan, the owner of the garage, a few months earlier. Mohan was an expert body repairman who could make almost any car look like new.

"What the heck did you do to your front end, Zeke?" he asked.

"Somebody backed into my truck while I was at Shaw's Market yesterday and obviously took off without so much as a note on my windshield. Probably has no insurance," Zeke responded. "This damned state. You might need insurance to get your car registered, but once you've got the registration, there's nothing to stop you from just cancelling the coverage. What you end up with is a whole bunch of uninsured cars on the road, ready to smash into somebody's vehicle and get away with it."

Frank eyed the truck as he scanned it from side to side.

"Looks like you'll need a new front bumper. I can probably bang it back for you to save money, Zeke, but you'll need to repaint the hood."

"You know what, Frank, how much to repaint the whole truck white instead?"

"Painting a light color over a dark one might mean several coats to do a good job. You'd be better off if I repainted it black. I could probably get away with less paint. With the work on the bumper, if I go with black paint, it should be around $600. Do you have coverage for uninsured motorist on your policy?"

"No, I can't afford it yet; maybe when I have more money saved up. Can I pay you $100 a week for six weeks?"

"We can work it out. When do you want this done?"

"As soon as possible, Frank. I need my truck to get to work in North Smithfield. I can get a ride for a couple of days, but not much more than that. I'm supposed to call the guy so he can pick me up from here. So, I'd rather leave the truck here now, if you don't mind?" Zeke answered.

"I can have the truck ready in three days. You can pick it up on Friday, but I'll need at least $200 by then, and $100 a week over the next four weeks. Is this okay? You can borrow that old Chrysler Concord over there for the next few days. This way you won't need to bum rides to get around."

Zeke was not taking any chances someone had seen the truck at the accident scene.

* * *

In an effort to lure the assailant to make a mistake, Chief Plasse had a plan. He would announce to the press that Bonnie Stevens was recuperating from an auto accident in

Landmark Medical Center and an investigation was under-
way since the police had reason to suspect Miss Stevens' car
had been deliberately run off the road. The chief would further announce she would be well enough to sit with a police
sketch artist to give a rendering of the suspect's face as she
remembered she saw him in her rearview mirror just before
impact with the grove of trees. The sketch might enable the
police to identify the assailant in the next few days.

All the while, the chief had made arrangements to pri-
vately move Bonnie to a more secure part of the hospital
where he would station two detectives in her room. In the
ICU unit she currently occupied, Plasse had arranged to
use a mannequin covered in bandages to hide the face,
and with a blanket covering the body up to the neck. The
mannequin would have simulated tubes and monitors connected to it, and the room lights would be dimmed to make
it difficult for anyone to realize the patient in the bed was
not a real person at all. Plasse would assign a uniformed
police officer outside the room, deliberately allowing him
to walk away from his post from time to time to see if anyone attempted to enter the room.

At nine o'clock that night, Zeke entered the hospital
from an open door leading to the maintenance area on
the lower level of the hospital. He snuck into a locker room
area and found some work clothes in one of the lockers.
He then grabbed a bucket on wheels and a mop, and made
his way toward the ICU unit on the third floor by way of the
service elevator.

Once on the third floor, he slowly made his way down
the corridor and searched for his prey, one room at a
time. His gun, with the silencer already placed at the end
of the barrel, was hidden on a tray under the bucket he

wheeled forward. In the distance, just around a corner on the adjacent wing of the floor, he could see a policeman stationed outside one of the rooms. He quickly grabbed a rag and a spray bottle attached to the bucket and made believe he was cleaning an area near one of the bathrooms. Occasionally, he looked back toward the policeman who suddenly headed in his direction. When the policeman walked right by him and around the corner, Zeke quickly looked back outside the room where he had been seated. There was no one else there.

Zeke grabbed his bucket and mop and began to approach the empty chair just vacated by the policeman. He looked into the room and saw a partially drawn curtain. He reached for his gun under the bucket, entered the amber lit room and fired several shots at the figure in the bed.

He then quickly left the room, looked both ways in the corridor, and pushed his mop and bucket back towards the service elevator. As he rounded the last corner, the police-man who had passed him earlier was returning to his post. Zeke lowered his head and kept on moving. The police-man didn't even glance his way. Zeke reached the elevator, pushed the down button, and descended back to the base-ment. He was out the maintenance door and on his way in the loaned Chrysler in less than five minutes.

The policeman returned to his station outside the patient doorway, but noticed the mannequin had moved. He flicked on the light switch and could see the bullet rid-dled bed. He grabbed his walkie-talkie and yelled into it.

"Secure all exits. We have a visitor in the house."

In a flash, he recalled the janitor who had passed him in the hallway. He dashed in that direction, but there was no one in sight.

"The service elevator, he took the service elevator."

Three detectives rushed toward the maintenance area in the basement of the hospital, and all they saw as they entered the locker room was a pile of workers' clothes, thrown next to a bucket and mop.

"Don't touch any of it," a detective yelled. "Maybe we'll find prints on the mop or the bucket. Maybe he wasn't wearing gloves."

Chief Plasse arrived at the hospital within minutes, and as he entered the hospital room where the mannequin had been placed, his eyes gazed at the bed.

"Whoa, this guy means business. We have a killer on our hands here. Not a word about this to anyone, is that clear? This young woman would be dead right now, and I don't want any announcement or discussion outside the department. Are we clear?"

"Mr. Strange, I'm glad I could reach you. This is Chief Plasse. Our little set up lured him here, but he managed to elude us. You were right, Mr. Strange, he was set on killing her. We'll beef up our protection and not allow any unapproved people to come anywhere near her room."

"If anything happens to Bonnie Stevens, Chief..." His voice drifted off.

"I understand, Mr. Strange. We won't let this happen, I promise you."

Over the next few days, Zeke frantically scanned the morning newspapers to read about any incident at the hospital, but there was nothing there. In his mind, no news was not good news. Had he failed to rid a threat to the Tates? Had she really seen his face before the crash?

Zeke had already decided once his parole time was over in the next few weeks, he would leave the area for a while to be out of harm's way. His past record and his ties to the Tates would surely place him squarely on the police's radar as a suspect in both cases. If he wasn't around, he couldn't be questioned, and he believed it would all die down in time. He would only return to the area when the time was right.

CHAPTER 14

The days that followed Samantha's experiences in Rhode Island were spent by Alex and her on the web in efforts to sort out the apparent past-life recollections by Samantha. The house in Cumberland, the law office of Michael Strange in Providence, and the news headlines from the Providence Journal at the Providence Public Library, all were bizarre occurrences Samantha did not understand, and Alex was more confused by all these events than he ever imagined.

Ironically, when they met the following weekend, both of them had separately read an article by Dr. K.S. Rawat on reincarnation, written in the March/April, 1997 issue of *Venture Inward Magazine.* The article focused on an Indian girl, Shanti Devi, who claimed to be Lugdi Bai in a past life. Lugdi Bai had died nine days after she had given birth to a son in 1925. In late 1926, Shanti Devi was born in a totally different location in India. At the very young age of four, Shanti began talking to her parents about "her husband" and "her children."

The more Shanti spoke in later years, the more she revealed information about another house in another city she had lived in with her husband. Shanti described the clothes she wore as Lugdi Bai, and the foods she ate. She would even describe to her parents how she had died in her previous life.

As Samantha went over this thorough account, she could not stop reading the story. She herself remembered a woman being murdered over twenty-two years earlier in 1989, the year she was born, a few months after the woman's murder. She had told Alex she now knew the murdered woman in her dreams was actually her in a previous life. Mike Strange had been her husband, and her name was Susan.

As she continued to read the story about Shanti Devi, she began to remember more and more information, as if she was in Rhode Island all over again. She remembered her parents, her teacher friends at the elementary school where she taught, and she even remembered Hawaii. There were things only Susan and Mike knew about each other and about their plans for the future. These things had not been discussed with others.

When Samantha met with Alex on Sunday afternoon, after the Wednesday episodes, they just gazed at each other at first, for just a moment, before Alex finally spoke.

"Sammy, when was the last time you mentioned to your folks about the dreams of the woman being murdered?" he asked.

"Not for some time now, Alex, why?"

"Because I think they need to know what's going on right now, especially after this past week."

"Alex, I think we should see this through a little longer, to see where it goes. I already feel much more relieved this stuff is coming out. It's like I turned a key in a locked closet, and when I opened the door, all of this stuff came pouring out."

"So, what's next?" Alex asked.

"Well, from what I've read about Susan Strange's murder, they never found the killer. She graduated from Northeastern in 1987, got married in 1988, and died in 1989. What if I volunteer to write an article about her for the college newspaper? They could call it *Unsolved Murder of Northeastern Graduate Is 22 Years Old.*

"What would you get from doing that?"

"It would allow me a chance to interview people who were close to the case. And maybe this would stir more flashbacks for me. Can you imagine if I could identify this killer after all this time? Mike Strange, his parents, and Susan's parents would like to see this case reopened, I bet?" she added.

"This is very sensitive stuff, Sammy. You may end up with some bad memories these people don't want to relive. Are you sure you want to go there?"

"Look, Alex, besides my parents, you're the only other person who knows what I am going through right now. And you know even more now than they do. You're the only one who can help me bring this to an end, once and for all. Besides, I don't think they would believe a word about what's happened in the last week. They still think it's some kind of sleep disorder."

"Well, I don't know where you'll begin with this. The husband, Mike Strange, or should I say your former husband, spends most of his time in Hawaii. You don't know if his parents or Susan's parents are still around. My guess is the best start is with the Cumberland Police Department. See what they have on the case," Alex replied.

"One of the editors of *The Huntington News* is Christine Ettoya, and she was in one of my education classes last semester. Let me run this by her this week. She lives in Arlington, just a couple of miles from their offices on Huntington Avenue. I'll stop by *The News* tomorrow and see if she comes in during the summer. If not, I can call her at home to run the idea by her."

"Alex, I'm scared about this. What if it's true? What if I really was Susan Strange in another life? What if I remember the guy who murdered me? What if I run into him on the street one day? What if I tell Mike Strange who I think I was back in 1989, and he thinks I'm nuts?"

"Honestly, I don't have a clue. I'm scared too right now, scared that we might find something and won't know how to handle it. You can't just go around saying you were someone else in your previous life. I've never really believed in reincarnation until I read about this Shanti Devi Indian woman and her story. All the stuff she knew about her other life was never refuted, and everything she said about the other life turned out to be true. She knew places and things no one ever told her before. She even knew how she died and remembered it. She knew her son, even though she only saw the child for less than nine days after he was born.

You can't just walk up to a guy and tell him you're his past wife who just came back from the dead. This is awful sensitive stuff. We are going to have to go very slow with this," Alex continued.

"Do I think you're nuts? Of course not, but a lot of others will. We can't let this become a side show for the media. If anyone gets wind of your story about a previous life, you'll have every whacko out there calling you a fraud. Talk about paparazzi, there would be no place for you to hide."

CHAPTER 15

On August 15ᵗʰ, Jonathan Tate walked into Mike Strange's office at ten o'clock in the morning. He had not made an appointment ahead of time. After he introduced himself to Mike, Jonathan was asked the reason for his visit without an appointment.

"Mr. Tate, as you are aware, our firm represents the families of twelve former residents of Rock Ridge Common who all died from lung cancer and all of whom never smoked a cigarette a day in their lives, nor worked in an environment where second-hand smoke was prevalent. As such, you should know I cannot talk to you about this law suit unless you are here to offer some kind of settlement to avoid a lengthy trial. Since I don't see a representative from your liability carrier here with you, I will assume you are not here to do that. And by the way, if I find that you had anything to do with my wife's murder, Mr. Tate, I will per-sonally see to it you never set foot out of prison. Because if you do, you'd better be ready to look over your shoulder every single day for the rest of your miserable life. Now, what the hell do you want?"

Jonathan's stunned look had him speechless for the moment as he tried to compose himself from Mike's tirade. He took a few deep breaths and began.

"Mr. Strange, I can understand your outrage at your wife's murder, and I can also understand you think I some-how had some responsibility in this terrible tragedy because it happened at the same time you became involved in the deaths of some former Rock Ridge residents," Jonathan said as he looked directly at Mike.

"Mr. Strange, I had nothing to do with the death of your wife. I don't know how I would react if something like this happened to my own wife. I'm not an evil man, Mr. Strange. I run a very successful homebuilding business with hun-dreds of satisfied homeowners. If this law suit you have proves to be successful against me, my insurance company will pay whatever damages are determined by the court. I'm here to see if we can come to some kind of settlement out-side the courtroom. Any bad press which comes out of this is bad for my business. Even if we win the case, it's not the kind of publicity we want."

"First off, Tate, I don't know you at all and I don't like you. Secondly, you don't have enough coverage in your insurance policy to cover the damages I'll be looking for at the trial. If my clients win this thing, you're going to have to come up with a lot more money. So, spare me the bullshit about your insurance company coverage. My guess is, if your insurance company finds out you submitted doctored engineering reports to the town, and to them, you may have a lot of explaining to do with Mutual of New England. Wait a minute. You're here because you gave Mutual of New England the false engineering report too, didn't you?" Mike gave a smirk to Jonathan.

"I don't know what report you're referring to, Mr. Strange. But I can assure you the report Mutual of New England has is the same one filed in the town records ten years ago," Jonathan replied.

"Do I look like I just got off the boat yesterday, Tate? We're not talking about the real Siteco report are we? We're not talking about the official report from Siteco which stated your land was loaded with radon, and they recommended you get rid of it?" Mike went on.

"What are you talking about? What official report are you referring to? There's only one report from Siteco, and it's the official report filed with the Town of North Smithfield and with Mutual of New England," Jonathan countered.

"Well, one of us is lying, Tate, and it sure as hell isn't me," Mike retaliated.

"Let's cut through this surprise act and this shocking discovery, and let's get to the real reason you're here today."

"It has been brought to my attention there may have been some things in the engineering report which were somehow left out when the report was filed. I was not aware that the grounds Rock Ridge sits on contained hazardous material, or I would have ordered the threat removed. My brother Jerry handled the site engineering phase while I handled the finances and the construction of the units. When Mutual of New England contacted us about the law suit you filed, I questioned my brother on it. At first, he said he knew of no problems in the engineering results from the site. But the more I pressed him on it, the weaker his argument became, until he finally mentioned the word radon. Mr. Strange, if our carrier finds out that the report they have from Siteco is false, they won't cover us on the law suit. Our coverage, as you know, is for ten million dollars. If we lose the case, and this is a big 'if", we're out of business, bankrupt. If that happens, your clients will probably end up with two million dollars tops, this is all we have without the insurance. Once you take your third, there'll only be a little over one hundred thousand dollars left per family. I'm willing to offer each family six hundred thousand dollars, over seven million dollars in total, payable in one hundred thousand dollar installments each year for the next six years. My brother and I will put up all of our own personal assets as collateral. The only stipulation is that the settlement be done in the next week, and without the insurance company's involvement. We need the ten million dollar coverage going forward for our other projects, and I'm afraid they may drop our coverage completely if the case goes to trial and they dispute the verification of the engineering report."

"I don't know if I believe your little story which pins all the blame on your brother, Tate. But, quite frankly, I don't care who points a finger at the other at this point. The damage is done. If you relied on his actions and honestly knew nothing about the radon problem, then your brother is a bigger fool than you. But he is your brother and a principal in Tate Builders, which makes him as negligent as you," Mike answered.

"I need the offer in writing, exactly as you've proposed. Then, and only then, will I ask my clients whether they wish to accept your offer or not," Mike continued.

"I'll have it here in your office by three o'clock today, Mr. Strange. I think you're making a smart move for your clients."

"Don't flatter yourself, you asshole, twelve people are dead because of Tate Builders, and whether the six hundred thousand dollars is enough for this to go away, is not up to me.

Jonathan Tate knew enough not to overstay his presence in Mike's office, and rose to leave.

"What happened was unfortunate, and I know it could have and should have been prevented. I have to live with the belief that those twelve people might be gone today because of our inaction," Jonathan said as he started toward the door.

"Might be gone because of you? Not one, not two, twelve, Tate, twelve innocent people who probably never knew what extensive exposure to radon could do," Mike replied.

"What if you and your wife had lived at Rock Ridge for the last ten years, Tate, and you developed lung cancer. Would you think that radon might have caused it if the levels were five times the acceptable level in your unit? It would have been a lot cheaper to fix it ten years ago, wouldn't it?"

As Jonathan left the law office and later arrived at his office, his phone rang. The voice at the other end spoke loudly and with emphasis.

"Mr. Tate, this is Rupert Kubaska from Mutual of New England. We just went over the law suit filed by Michael Strange and Associates on behalf of twelve families claiming wrongful deaths due to overexposure to radon gas, which they say caused their family member to get lung cancer. Do you have a minute?"

"Sure."

"Mr. Tate, if you lose this case, I'm not certain your coverage of ten million will be enough. The good news is, if they win this case on circumstantial evidence, it will be the first radon case to do so. Even if you knew there was radon there ten years ago, there are no laws out there which state you have to do something about it. Our team of attorneys here believes it can easily win this case or even get it thrown out of court even before it starts. We don't believe there is clear-cut evidence that connects any of the victims to radon induced lung cancer. No one has yet determined how much exposure is too much exposure, no one. So, I wouldn't worry too much about this, Mr. Tate. We'll be talking soon."

Once Kubaska hung up the phone, Jonathan sat back in his chair and smiled. He wondered, *"Well, well, I just may not be back there this afternoon after all."*

CHAPTER 16

"I like the idea, Samantha. The thought of revisiting a tragedy still unsolved after twenty-two years is not your usual college newspaper story. But the fact it happened to a Northeastern grad makes it all the more intriguing. Where will you begin, and what's your target date for the article?" Christine Ettoya asked when Samantha dropped in on Monday morning on August 22.

"Alex thinks I should work with the Cumberland police department where they have all the records on the case. I can probably get the parents' addresses from them, and even find out when the husband is back in town. He spends most of his time now in Maui. To my knowledge, I don't think he ever remarried," answered Samantha.

"Sounds great. Keep me posted on how you're doing. I'm thinking the November issue if it's not too soon for you?"

"Okay. Let's set it as my goal. I'll try to have a draft to you by mid-September. I'll even try to include current photos of the parents. I doubt the husband will be around for pictures."

The following day, Samantha called Alex to see if he wanted to accompany her to the police station on Wednesday. She had already called the Cumberland police and was told Sergeant Lemoine would meet with her at ten o'clock that day.

"Of course, I'll go. I'll pick you up at nine o'clock."

As they drove the same route to Rhode Island they had driven a few weeks earlier, Samantha felt an eerie feeling as she thought carefully at the questions she would ask Sgt. Lemoine. Sgt. Ed Lemoine was a thirty-year veteran of the Cumberland police at age fifty-two. In 1989, he had been the first detective to respond to the 911 call from Gordie Landry. This incident was his first as a detective, having just been elevated from squad car duty a week earlier.

"Ed Lemoine, please," Samantha said to the clerk at the desk as she and Alex entered the police station on High Street.

Ed was a huge man at six feet five inches tall and muscles bulging from his arms like a local Rambo. But underneath the picture perfect frame laid a man as gentle as could be. His reputation as a hard line interrogator was developed by his constant and incessant ability to persuade perpetrators to confess to crimes they had committed. His calm demeanor and convincing approach to solving cases was very effective. Nevertheless, when he approached Samantha and Alex in the lobby, both of them looked up in awe at his size, despite the warm smile on his face.

"Miss Collins, I presume. I'm Sgt. Lemoine. Welcome to Cumberland. And this is?" he asked looking directly at Alex.

"Oh, I'm sorry, Sgt. Lemoine. This is my friend, Alex Brien, also from Northeastern."

"Nice to meet you, Alex. Well, shall we get started? I've got the file box on the Susan Strange case in one of the conference rooms. I thought we would work in there. I can tell you as much as I know about that day, but, unfortunately, we never really had a solid lead to go on."

Lemoine led them to a second floor conference room. As they entered, Samantha was surprised to see how little information the police had in the file. The event was now considered a cold case since there had not been any new information on the murder in several years.

"We never really got to first base on this case. No one came forward with the identity of the cable truck and driver seen on the street that day. When we recovered the stolen Venture truck a few days later, forensics found no traces of anything in it. The truck had been wiped clean. There were no signs of forced entry, no indications of sexual molestation, no indications of a robbery when the husband reported nothing missing, pretty much a dead end," Lemoine began.

"The husband, Mike Strange, kept insisting the shooting was related to the law suit he was working on against Tate Builders, but we could never find the connection. They both had alibis for their whereabouts on the day of the murder, and the alibis held up. It's possible they, the Tate brothers, could have hired someone to do their dirty work, but again we could never prove any of this."

"I take it the killer didn't leave any clues at the murder scene? No finger prints anywhere, no cigarette butts, and shell casings, none of that stuff?" Alex asked.

"Ironically, this shooter was calm. We found an empty glass on the counter, but he must have worn gloves, and we found no prints on the glass at all. I said 'he', but for all we know it could have been a woman, or someone she knew and not the mysterious cable guy. I doubt that because of the recovered Venture truck just two days later."

"What about the motive of a robbery gone badly?" Samantha asked.

"I don't think so, Miss Collins. The struggle was only in the living room area where she died. No other room had anything out of place, no drawers open, no ransacking anywhere. I still think it was a poor attempt to make it look like a break-in gone badly, especially if you're going to take the time to pour yourself a drink. Unless the beverage was from before the shooting, indicating Mrs. Strange was unsuspecting if she offered the shooter a drink. I still don't think it was just a random act, but I could never get a lead in the case," Lemoine went on.

"Funny thing though, Mike Strange calls me at least once a month to see if anything's come up. He never went on with his life socially after his wife's murder. He even calls me from Hawaii where he lives most of the year. His condo in Berkshire Estates is usually empty most of the time. A broken man I tell you."

"This box contains interviews with several neighbors, the husband, and even one with the Tate brothers. Feel free to go through it, but you can't take anything with you. You can take photocopies or notes. Heck, maybe you'll find something we missed. If I can be of more assistance, just dial extension 240."

"Sergeant, do you know if Susan's parents are still alive, and Mike's too?" Samantha asked.

"I believe so. Susan's parents still live in Pawtucket. He was a cop there, you know, Susan's father, Ralph Pennington. Mike's dad is still alive too, but he's in a retirement home in Lincoln, a little dementia I heard. I'll get you their addresses."

Lemoine rose and excused himself from the room. Samantha and Alex then began sifting through the files and took notes on anything they thought would become information for the article. When she came across a photo of Susan Strange's dead body, Samantha could not stop staring at the photo. She did not let Alex see her expression and quickly flipped the photo over and continued to the next piece of information in the file.

Shortly after noon, she dialed Lemoine's extension and thanked him for his help. Lemoine read out the parents' addresses to Samantha and told her to leave the file box in the conference room and he would retrieve it later. There was no rush, in his mind, since the file was going back into the cold case bin in the basement of the station.

They left Cumberland at two o'clock after grabbing a bite at the nearest Dunkin Donuts down the street. They drove toward Central Street in Pawtucket. Samantha had a queasy feeling at the thought of her visit to Susan's parents. *What if I recognize them and realize they were my parents years ago?* She pondered. *What if I get emotional in front of them and they stare at me and wonder why I'm acting this way?* These thoughts stayed fresh in her mind as they approached the Pennington house.

CHAPTER 17

"Alex, I know this house. This is where I was brought up. Maybe this is not such a good idea."

"Sammy, you've come this far for a reason. You have to see this through, or you will always wonder what's inside this house. It's time to find out more, once and for all," Alex answered.

They walked up the driveway and rang the doorbell. As the front door opened, an older woman appeared and looked at them with a serious look on her face.

"Can I help you?" Alice asked.

"I'm sorry to bother you, ma'am, but we are students from Northeastern University doing an article for the school newspaper about the death of Susan Pennington Strange twenty-two years ago. Are you Mrs. Pennington?" Alex asked.

"Yes, I am. You say you are doing a story about Susan? Oh, my, I don't know if I want to talk about her death. It's been so long now," Alice answered.

"Mrs. Pennington, my name is Samantha Collins, and this is my friend, Alex Brien. We realize this may be difficult for you, but it's been so long since she was murdered, and the killer still has never been found. She was the only Northeastern graduate who was ever murdered. We thought the article would be of interest to other Northeastern students, and maybe the local newspapers might run the story too."

"Would you please wait here? I'll ask my husband if he wants anything to do with this," she said.

"Please tell Mr. Pennington that Sgt. Lemoine sent us," Alex added before Alice closed the front door.

A few minutes later, Ralph appeared at the door.

"You say Ed Lemoine sent you?"

"Yes, we were just there a short while ago, and reviewed the file on your daughter's case," Alex commented.

"Ed's a good guy. Please, come in," Ralph said with a tone of enthusiasm in his voice. When they entered the living room of the house, Alex glanced at Samantha and noticed tears running down her cheek as she quickly wiped them away before anyone else noticed them.

"Let's sit out back on the screened-in porch. It gets too stuffy in here in the summer, and the air conditioner makes too much noise when it's on and you're trying to have a conversation."

Ralph was about to lead them in the direction of the screened-in porch when he saw Samantha instinctively heading directly through the kitchen to the porch without hesitation. Ralph looked at her quizzically, wondering how she knew the way. He kept his thoughts to himself, however, as he asked them to be seated.

"So, Samantha and Alex, why the sudden interest in my daughter's murder after all these years?" Ralph's police curiosity had the best of him. At the same time, Alice appeared with a tray of lemonade and four glasses, and sat next to Ralph on the settee facing the young couple.

"Each year, the newspaper looks at news that was in the current month's issue twenty or more years earlier to see if there may be an update worth mentioning. We call it *Twenty Plus Years Ago.* The story about your daughter's murder was published in 1989, and we wondered what happened since then," Samantha mentioned.

She looked away from Ralph as she spoke, which puzzled him. Instead, she was totally fixated on Alice and could not take her eyes off of her.

"Is there some reason you are staring at me?" Alice asked.

"Oh, I'm so sorry. You remind me of someone, and I'm trying to remember who," Samantha answered.

"Have we met before?" Alice asked.

"I don't think so. I'm from New Jersey and this is only the second time in my life in Rhode Island."

"You're just about the same size as Susan was years ago. We were very close and spent a lot of time together. Her husband, Mike, was so busy trying to build his law practice that he worked long hours at the office. Susan had much more time to herself, and since we were both teachers, our schedules allowed us to grab lunch or go shopping pretty often."

"Did Susan ever want to be a college professor like you, and maybe teach at Brown?" Samantha asked.

"No, I don't think so. And how did you know I taught at Brown?" Alice asked with a puzzled look on her face.

"Oh, I must have read it somewhere before we came here," Samantha fumbled for words.

"Perhaps you read it from one of the newspaper articles from 1989?" Alice commented.

"Your daughter and you were very close then?" Samantha asked as tears swelled in her eyes.

"We were best friends. Our conversations were about anything and everything. She talked about raising a family with Mike, and how wonderful it would be for me to become a grandmother. Did you know when they did her autopsy, they found she was pregnant? So much for being a grandmother," Alice mentioned as she stared solemnly toward the back yard beyond the porch.

"That wasn't public knowledge, was it?"

"No, only Ralph and I and Mike were told about it by the police."

"Mr. Pennington, when you started looking into Susan's death with Sgt. Lemoine, you suspected the Tate brothers had something to do with it, didn't you?" Alex asked.

"I still feel that way today. Those bastards have made millions from a condo development built on a health hazard property which sits on a huge amount of radon gas underground. A lot of people died from cancer because the Tates didn't seal the foundations which allowed the gas to infiltrate a lot of basements in the condo units. Back then, there weren't too many rules which prevented this. They could never get away with it today. Susan's husband, Mike, was suing the Tates for millions, and I just know they tried to get to Mike by going after Susan. She never hurt a fly, and Mike hasn't been the same after all these years, neither have we."

"Sgt. Lemoine told us that the Tates had alibis that day," Alex added.

"This doesn't mean they didn't get somebody else to do the job," Ralph emphasized. "We just couldn't connect anybody else to the Tates back then."

"If, by some luck, we find something new on the case, Mr. Pennington, is it safe to say they would re-open the case?" Alex asked.

"In my mind, young man, the case will always be open until we find out who killed her," Ralph answered.

"Thank you for meeting with us and for being so kind. We'll be sure to send you a copy of the article when it comes out in November. We are going to try to talk to Mr. Strange's father next," Samantha said.

"I'm not so sure that will get you anywhere. Carl Strange is not well. His wife, Linda, died about five years ago, and since then his mind started slipping. He is borderline Alzheimer's right now. He may not even know what you're talking about," Ralph commented. Alice agreed.

"That's a shame. Mike Strange, we were told, lives most of the year in Hawaii, and only spends time here in Rhode Island around Christmas. I'm afraid the article needs to be done by mid-September and we won't be able to talk directly to him in time," Samantha added.

"I don't think that's accurate, Samantha. Mike is scheduled to be in town Labor Day weekend. He still has his law firm and is scheduled to meet some new clients on Tuesday, September 6th, right after the holiday. He's supposed to call us for dinner the weekend before. He emailed us about a week ago so we wouldn't make any other plans for the weekend. Not that we do much traveling anymore," Ralph answered.

"You wouldn't share his email address with us by any chance, would you?" Alex asked.

"I'll tell you what. You leave me your email addresses and I'll check with Mike if he wants me to give it out. He's a very private person and, other than Bonnie, he doesn't socialize very much," Ralph added.

"Bonnie. Who's Bonnie?" Samantha asked.

"She is just about the only close friend he talks to. She was his paralegal when Susan was murdered, and she almost died too after being run off the road working on the radon case. So you think the two weren't related incidents? Mike still blames himself for this whole mess."

"Does she still work at the firm?"

"No, but she'll be here with Mike in a couple of weeks. Although Mike never remarried, he and Bonnie became very close back then after all of this happened, and I don't know why they never married," Alice chimed in. "She is a lovely person and they live together in Hawaii."

"Say, Mrs. Pennington, this may sound a bit forward, but would you give me a quick tour of the house? I think we may be in the market for one soon and this is very nice."

Alex looked at Samantha with a surprised look on his face, a look which he had too often expressed lately.

"Are you two a couple?" asked Alice.

"Well, sort of, I guess. We've talked some about after graduation next year, and one thing led to another," Samantha answered with a glow on her face.

As they rose from the porch, Samantha picked up the empty glasses and walked for the kitchen area where she placed them on the counter, all the while scanning from side to side.

"This is Susan's room, pretty much the same as when she went off to Northeastern in the mid-80s," Alice said with a sigh as they entered the room at the end of the hall.

Samantha began to cry, almost uncontrollably, as she entered. Alice saw the tears flowing down her cheek and immediately went to her.

"Oh, my dear, what's wrong?" she asked.

"I'm so sorry, Mrs. Pennington. The room looks exactly like my own room back in New Jersey. Except for the posters on the wall being different, the rest is the same. I feel like I know you more than you can imagine."

"I often break down myself when I come in here. I just can't seem to control myself either. Come, let's go back to see the men on the porch," Alice answered as she held Samantha around the shoulders.

The ride back to Boston was less than quiet.

"Alex, Alice Pennington was my mother, and Ralph was my father. I'm sure of this. Setting foot in that house was bizarre. I lived there for nearly twenty years before, and I don't have a clue how this can happen. I keep remembering more and more each time I revisit this Susan thing. I hope we get a chance to meet Mike Strange when he's here in a couple of weeks. Maybe then, and not before, all of this will go away."

They pulled into the parking lot for La Mâison Henri at six o'clock and were greeted by Alex's parents. They took a table in the far corner of the restaurant and exchanged pleasantries until the parents were needed elsewhere in the restaurant as patrons slowly entered for dinner on this Wednesday evening.

"Sammy, were you just making small talk at the Pennington house about looking at houses, or did I miss something along the way?" Alex asked.

"I guess a little of both, Alex. I'm very confused right now, as if I'm leading two lives, and yet you stick with me through it all. I've never met anyone like you before, and I don't think I could talk to anyone else the way I've opened up to you. So, I guess what I told Mrs. Pennington is what I hope can happen between us someday."

"Samantha Collins, if you were Susan Strange before, you're not now. Who you may have been before is really weird and nothing I've ever heard of until now. But I don't have any better answers than you do, and I've seen your reaction with my own eyes when these episodes have occurred. I don't like this happening to you, but I don't love you any less because of it. This restaurant will belong to me someday, and we can have a really nice life together, Sammy."

On this night, Samantha and Alex had the most passionate love experience they had ever had together. But Alex knew the drill that followed. As he was about to get dressed to go home, as had always been the case before, Samantha this time pulled him back into her bed and asked him to stay the night with her. If her dreams of the past came calling this night, she wanted Alex there. It was time for him to see for himself.

CHAPTER 18

Jonathan Tate was a complicated man. In his early twenties, he had mastered handling most pieces of heavy equipment used in earth moving. When he approached the age of thirty, he thought he was ready for greater things beyond heavy equipment operation, and he began building homes. At first, because of the limited funds he had at his disposal, his focus was on smaller ranch houses and raised ranches, very much similar to what his father had built in the early 1960s, and where Jonathan had learned the trade.

He met his wife Helen at a local dance club in 1975. Helen Goodman was an operating room nurse at Rhode Island Hospital. She had seen how hard her parents struggled to raise her and her younger brother, Zeke, in cheap, dilapidated housing in South Providence, and swore she would someday take her parents away from the area when she finished her studies in nursing school. True to her word, in 1978 she bought a charming three-bedroom home in Scituate, a rural community north of Providence, and shared the home with her retired parents who had spent most of their adult lives in the sweat shops of the Pawtucket textile mills, and had little to show for it.

Jonathan would tell Helen how he one day would be a rich man, and how he wanted to raise a family on an estate he planned to build in Glocester, close to where she lived. The radon lawsuit, in his mind, was a mere stumbling block on his rise to fame and fortune in the home construction business. He truly believed cutting corners here and there in the homebuilding field was the difference between failure and success. *If it's not required,* he would say, *then it can be eliminated.* This was the approach he had taken with the engineering report in 1980, and would likely be the same approach he would use with deceiving town officials with false promises of amenities in most of his projects.

Mike Strange had put together a solid case against Tate Builders. His rage at being suckered in to believing Jonathan would make good on his settlement offer to the plaintiffs made him all the more angry and determined to win the case. The trial was set to begin in October, 1989, and Mike spent the bulk of his time either getting the case ready for trial, or working with the Cumberland police to find Susan's killer. Either way, Jonathan Tate and his brother were involved. Mike was certain of this.

Bonnie Stevens had regained consciousness from the head injuries suffered from the car crash earlier in the summer, and Mike was relieved to see her sitting up in her bed at Landmark Medical Center on Wednesday morning in mid-August when he visited her this day. As he held her hand while standing beside her bed, he felt the instant warmth that emanated from her smile as she welcomed the gesture. Other than perhaps a neighbor from her condo complex in the Kirkbrae section of Lincoln, Bonnie did not expect to get too many visitors during her recovery. So the visit by Mike was the highlight of her day.

Doctors had reported to Mike that Bonnie would make a full recovery and would be released by the end of the week. North Smithfield police were now more concerned than ever at her safety. Zeke Goodman was still considered a threat, even though the police were not aware of his existence, and he had suddenly disappeared from the area on Jonathan's insistence until the trial was over.

* * *

Rupert Kubaska, the head trial lawyer for Mutual of New England who had been assigned the case against Tate Builders, stared out the window of his office on the eighteenth floor of the Prudential Building in Boston. On this late night, Rupert could look out at the barren darkness from other offices, with only the glimmer of lights from Fenway Park in the distance. He was sixty years old, and lived most nights during trial preparation in the insurance company's apartment, a short walk from the Pru.

Although he doubted the judge assigned to this trial, Judge Cromwell, would allow a motion to dismiss the case, he filed the motion anyway. In just a few short weeks, jury selection would begin, and Rupert never expected to see Michael Strange get this far. But as he glanced at his nearby conference table, he could see the piles of files on radon cases. Some had been settled in favor of the victims, but most had been summarily dismissed due to lack of sufficient proof that radon had been the cause of injury or death.

Next to these files were files which held medical records of the twelve deceased victims, their oncology history, chemotherapy and radiation treatment, and yearly medical checkups from as far back as twenty years prior to lung cancer diagnosis. Included with these were countless depositions taken from the surviving relatives of the Rock Ridge victims, most of which he had not read yet, and really didn't care to.

He clearly was not prepared to try the case, although he was still convinced there was insufficient evidence to warrant a finding for the plaintiffs. When his first request for a continuance had been denied in early August, Rupert decided to try again. He hoped a delay would hurt the plaintiffs' attorney, Mike Strange. He knew Strange was a sole practitioner with limited resources. The longer the delay before a trial, the tougher it would be for Strange to continue to practice with virtually no other current income stream to support his practice.

Rupert asked this time for a postponement of five months due to the massive amount of medical, technical, and engineering materials which needed to be reviewed in such a short time. If he succeeded in persuading the judge, Mike knew he could not afford to continue. The case was costing him more money than he made from smaller settlements, and he would have difficulty in just meeting payroll costs for Bonnie and one associate, as well as any outside use of investigators besides his father-in-law, Ralph.

At the pretrial conference in early September, 1989, Mike and Rupert Kubaska met with Judge Cromwell.

"Five more months before a trial?" exclaimed the judge, looking up from the request for continuance. "That's a long delay for the defense to request."

Mike, at this juncture, decided to become more aggressive once he felt the reluctance of the judge to delay the trial. "The plaintiffs are prepared to go forward as scheduled, Your Honor. We've been working day and night for months now. Mr. Kubaska has had the same amount of time as us. I don't see why we should be penalized because he is not ready, considering also he has so many more resources at his disposal than I do."

It was clear that Kubaska had taken the case for granted, and even had expected the case to be thrown out of court for insufficient proof of damage by the defendants. Kubaska had almost assured Jonathan earlier the case would be disallowed.

"How about we empanel the jury in the next couple of weeks," the judge said. "Then we commence trial in November instead of October. Does that work for you?"

Kubaska said quietly, "I'm going to have to put a lot more of my staff on this. It's very disappointing not to give me more time, Your Honor."

"Have the two of you discussed the possibility of a settlement?" asked the judge. "I'm assuming you both would welcome this to be settled without a lengthy trial."

"On August 15, Mr. Jonathan Tate came to my office and offered to settle for a total of $7.2 million, $600,000 to each victim's family, payable in $100,000 installments to each annually for the next six years. I asked him for the offer to be in writing, because I had no reason to believe his offer was genuine since he was not in the company of his insurance counsel at the time. Mr. Tate assured me he would have such an offer in writing on his letterhead and signed by him by three o'clock on the same day. He didn't show up, Your Honor, and has failed to return my phone calls on numerous occasions. He has also not responded to, nor accepted, my certified letters," Mike stated as he spoke directly to Judge Cromwell.

"Is this true, Mr. Kubaska? Were you aware of this?" asked the judge.

"I am not aware of any such offer by my client, Your Honor," Kubaska answered.

"Then I suggest you contact Mr. Tate today, Mr. Kubaska, and find out if he made such an offer. Are we clear on this?"

"Oh, by the way Rupert, you might inform your client I have his offer on tape. Whether the tape is admissible in court or not, you should be aware of what kind of a client you're representing. There are signs posted throughout my offices that all conversations will be recorded. Anyone willing to compromise someone's health for the sake of saving a few bucks on a condo project, would think nothing of reneging on an offer to settle," Mike stated with conviction as his comments were meant for the judge to hear as much as Kubaska.

"If, indeed, Mr. Tate made such an offer to Mr. Strange for the plaintiffs, Rupert, it's a far cry from the twelve million his clients are now suing for, isn't it?" the judge added.

"I'll give you until the weekend to talk to your client, Rupert. In the meantime, I will decide whether Mr. Strange's tape of his conversation with Mr. Tate would be allowed if the case is not settled before trial. I think it's time you get to know your client a little better."

* * *

The sun began to set as Mike left the courtroom that day. He walked briskly down Canal Street toward the parking lot. He had survived Kubaska's continuance request, much in the same way he had earlier survived summary judgment and discovery. He was elated at the results of the judge's conference and decided to forgo any celebration just yet. Instead, he decided to drive directly to Landmark Medical Center to visit Bonnie to share the news, and to see firsthand how her recuperation was coming along. She had earned the right to know how the case was proceeding. She had nearly paid the ultimate sacrifice.

"What do you think Tate will do, Mike?" asked Bonnie as she heard the news.

"I'm not sure, Bonnie. But you should have seen Kubaska's look when I told him about Tate's settlement offer. You would have thought he had just seen a ghost. He was even more surprised when I told him the conversation was all on tape."

"The doctors said I might be released tomorrow. The police are going to assign some people to watch my place while I'm still in danger. They don't even have a suspect yet. I don't know how long they think they can do this, but I'm a little scared to go home alone right now."

Mike could sense the anxiety in Bonnie's voice as she turned her head away from him to avoid him seeing the expression on her face.

"What time do you think they'll release you tomorrow?"

"Around three o'clock, they said."

"I'll swing by just before three and I'll take you home. If you don't mind some company for a while, I'll stick around. I can pick up a pizza or something later on from Cumberland House of Pizza. I think you could use a nice glass of pinot noir or a cabernet by then. Unless someone else is picking you up.

"No, just some detective from North Smithfield," Bonnie answered as she beamed a smile through her still badly bruised face.

As he left the hospital, Mike could only wonder. *How I'd love to be a fly on the wall in the meeting between Kubaska and Jonathan Tate.*

CHAPTER 19

Kubaska walked over to the credenza in his office, reached in the bottom drawer, and pulled out a bottle of Jim Beam bourbon whiskey. He reached for a glass on top of the credenza, threw in a few ice cubes from the ice bucket, and poured himself a generous amount. His mind was on the upcoming meeting with Jonathan Tate in a half hour at six o'clock. Rupert had been embarrassed by Mike in front of Judge Cromwell, a rare occurrence for him throughout his legal career. He didn't like it, but he blamed himself. He had been too casual at the pretrial conference, and for a brief moment, got blindsided by his own client's stupidity.

Rupert was not as concerned with the fact Jonathan's offer was on tape as he was at the offer being made without his knowledge in the first place. He believed he could have the offer thrown out as evidence since Jonathan had not been told directly his conversation with Mike was taped. Signs posted in Mike's office would not be sufficient grounds to allow Mike to play the tape before a jury. Rupert would argue it is easy to miss these notices, and only a direct verbal acknowledgment of the conversation on tape would be accepted by the court.

What bothered Rupert was Jonathan's offer to settle without consulting him first. Why would your own client do this? He would soon find out. Rupert's secretary buzzed him to inform him of Jonathan's arrival.

As Jonathan entered the office, Rupert spoke first.

"Jonathan, thank you for coming on such short notice. Can I pour you a bourbon?"

"Sure. I was surprised to hear from you this afternoon, but it sounded urgent, so here I am," Jonathan answered.

"There was a pretrial conference with Judge Cromwell today and Mike Strange had some interesting information I thought we should discuss. Have a seat."

"Fire away, Rupert, I've got nothing to hide," Jonathan replied with a cocky smile on his face.

"Well, that really is the problem, Jonathan. You do have something to hide, and you didn't do a very good job of hiding it."

"What do you mean?"

"I mean, when you make a seven million dollar offer to settle out of court, you really should know what the hell you're doing."

"Is that what Strange said? I made no such offer to him."

"Rule number one, Jonathan, is to never lie to your attorney or you won't have him for too long. Rule number two is to know when your conversation is on tape. So, spare me the bullshit and tell me now why you made such an offer to Strange without telling me. As a matter of fact, why would you offer to settle with your own money when you have an insurance company for that purpose?"

"Rupert, I need continued coverage from your company throughout this entire condo project, and hopefully, for the next projects we decide to tackle. If I lose your coverage, I'll never get financing from my bank."

"And why would you lose coverage from us, Jonathan?" Rupert asked with a puzzled look on his face.

"Suppose the engineering report on Rock Ridge was altered when it was filed in the town ten years ago. Suppose my stupid, asshole, brother omitted from Siteco's report certain things about radon gas on the property. Suppose he never told me he did this until a couple of weeks ago, and we would look foolish when the real Siteco report is shown in court. We would be guilty of hiding a health hazard from potential buyers for personal gain. I was afraid Mutual would stop handling the case because we filed erroneous reports with you as well back then. I thought if we lost coverage from you, which we might have, no other company would agree to cover us once they found out we gave you false reports. So, it made sense to try to settle this thing ourselves over a period of six years. Expensive, yes, but we'd still have coverage going forward."

"Stupidity must run in the family, Jonathan. You can't make an offer to an attorney to settle a case, and then never get back to him after he accepts your offer."

"When you called me in the afternoon a while back and told me the case would be easily won on our behalf, I saw no reason to go through with my offer."

"Fortunately for you, you moron, I think I can get the tape of your offer thrown out because he personally didn't say you were being recorded. You're not expected to read signs posted throughout his law office," Rupert added.

"As far as filing a false report ten years ago, when you signed the application for coverage with us, you believed at the time all the information to be true to the best of your knowledge. In other words, you had no knowledge of your brother's dealings at that time. Is this correct?"

"As God is my witness, Rupert, I only found out about this a couple of weeks ago, right before you called."

"So, in essence, you're asking me to continue your coverage with us, not only on this case, but throughout the project and then on subsequent projects. Mutual has settled several big cases this year, Jonathan, and this one may end up beating them all if we lose, even though I don't think we will lose," Rupert went on.

"The CEO here might not take any more losses too lightly. We might have to increase premiums or sell company investments to pay for any new settlements. He might think I'm not doing my job, Jonathan, and I'm about to have four years of college tuition for my daughter at Harvard starting next month. Where would I get this money from, Jonathan, if I lose my job? Do you understand my dilemma here? I'm talking about at least one hundred thousand dollars. Where would I get this money from? Before we go on, do we understand each other here?" Rupert asked.

"Are we saying you would continue on this case in exchange for added consideration on my part?" Jonathan replied.

"I'm just saying there are extenuating circumstances where a show of good faith would go a long way, especially one in cash in the one hundred thousand area, preferably untraceable bills."

Jonathan was caught in a very precarious position and Rupert knew he had him over a barrel. He was very confident he could win the law suit and save Mutual tens of millions in the process. This would bode well for his status in the company. But Jonathan's offer to settle, the false engineering report filed with the town, and the erroneous information on the application for coverage with Mutual, all of these were blackmail items Rupert could use. In his mind, Jonathan saw the one hundred thousand dollar bribe as acceptable, considering the alternatives.

They agreed to make the exchange on Tuesday of the following week in the parking lot of Vermette's Restaurant in Woonsocket. Rupert would be in the area attending the retirement party of an attorney on his staff that night. If he slipped outside the restaurant into the parking lot around seven o'clock, just for a brief moment, no one would even notice. He would stash the money under the front seat of his car. Later that night, on his ride back to Boston, Rupert decided to store the money in his office wall safe.

The trial would go on as scheduled.

CHAPTER 20

Judge Cromwell was always carefully involved in the selection of a jury. Normally, the process comprised of fifty or more people in his courtroom. But for this trial, he chose to have individual interviews of each prospective juror in his chambers. Although lawyers from both sides would be present, the judge alone would select the twelve jurors.

Ideally, Mike Strange hoped his jury would consist of twelve widows or widowers, or the son or daughter of a parent who recently died. For Rupert Kubaska, he preferred a juror with no past history of spousal or parental death. Judge Cromwell posed the same questions to all the prospective jurors. Were they aware of the causes of lung cancer? Had anyone in their family died from cancer? Had any family member lived in North Smithfield? Had any known about the dangers of radon in a residence? Had any read anything about this case?

The judge explained the circumstances of the case and the blame laid on the building contractor for omitting information about a potential health hazard from buyers of condominium units at Rock Ridge Common. Did each juror have a problem with viewing evidence and keeping an open mind with such evidence?

While some potential jurors were not favored by Kubaska, he waited for his right to use his six peremptory challenges on these. There were people who did not trust contractors to divulge information about property they sold, and who had no regard for environmental issues. Obviously, some potential jurors said anything that might get them excused from jury service. Others meant what they said and were generally excused.

Mike regretted losing certain candidates who appeared clearly to favor his side. But Kubaska felt the same way, especially when he lost the wife of another building contractor. At first, the judge thought she was a full-time mother of three young children, which she was. However, through questions that followed, it became apparent she favored all workers in the building trade. When Judge Cromwell asked her why she seemed to believe contractors were all very reputable people, she replied. "Well, Your Honor, my husband is a good man, hard-working, and very reputable. He too is a building contractor, much smaller than Tate, but he hopes to one day become as big as them." The woman was excused.

In all, it took nearly a week to select six jurors and six alternates. Mike and Rupert had each exhausted their six peremptory challenges and the final selection of three women and three men included two widows and a widower, a young housewife, a union plumber, and a certified public accountant. The ordeal had been very tiring to Mike who solely sat through these interviews while Rupert had several staff attorneys to assist him. Mike could see the advantage of a reliable support group by his side, but his lone associate had to remain in the office to handle other cases they had in the pipeline. With Bonnie still recuperating at home, Mike envied the size of Rupert's entourage from the insurance company. This made him all the more determined to focus on each jury candidate presented.

Judge Cromwell met early the next week with both Mike and Rupert to go over his idea of a trial plan. Because the suit involved two issues, the violation of withholding information of a potential health hazard from future owners, and the medical experts' testimony explaining how exposure to radon caused lung cancer in the victims, Judge Cromwell believed this approach would lessen the need to call twelve separate families to the stand to discuss somewhat the same two issues each time.

Mike liked the judge's approach, and so did Rupert. The first stage of the trial, the judge announced to the lawyers, would deal with whether Tate Builders was responsible for concealing the presence of radon from buyers of condominium units at Rock Ridge Common.

"Unless the jury finds Tate liable," said the judge, "there will be no point in going on. If the jury decides that Tate is liable, then you have to ask, 'Did the omission of corrective action contribute to the death of these twelve victims?'" Judge Cromwell shook his head as he pondered his own question.

CHAPTER 21

The next month for Mike was spent in preparation for the November trial. A jury had been selected, and expert witnesses had also been determined by both sides. Local attention by the press in Providence focused on the absence of clear Rhode Island law on the radon issue. The laws typically required disclosure of conditions which the seller of property is aware of or has knowledge to. These laws did not require the seller to undertake special investigation of any property to determine whether a condition existed. It was not possible to know the radon level of a specific property without conducting radon tests.

Both Mike Strange and Rupert Kubaska were aware of the vague territory they were in with regard to radon levels and any health hazard radon imposed. Convincing jurors either way would be a challenge for both attorneys. To

Mike, it meant millions of dollars in payments to survivors of the victims, small consolation for the loss of loved ones. To Rupert, it was more about the ego, the need to prove his worth, not only to his client Tate Builders, but the opportunity to make a better name for himself at Mutual of New England. Following the poor results at the pre-trial conference, Rupert took the case more seriously and surrounded himself with a team of attorneys from Mutual to solidify his client's position.

On the evening before the trial, Mike visited Bonnie at her home. Bonnie was now walking with the help of a cane, and her facial cuts and bruises were healing well. Mike began to now see how attractive she was, something he clearly never paid attention to before Susan's death.

"Good luck tomorrow, Mike. This is going to be a long trial. I wish I could be there with you. The police are still not convinced I should be in public yet. They have absolutely no leads, and they're afraid the driver may still be in the area waiting for another crack at me, no pun intended," she said with a smirk on her face.

Mike smiled as he could definitely notice Bonnie in good spirits. Perhaps it was because she did not get too many visitors, or perhaps she just enjoyed Mike's company.

The rest of the night Mike went over his opening statement for the jury. He had never tried such a huge case before, and he was very nervous. Several deep breaths between sections of his presentation helped his composure. At ten o'clock, he was ready for bed, knowing all too well this would likely be a sleepless night.

Judge Cromwell was in his office at the courthouse late before the scheduled trial was to begin. He hoped to hear from the two parties involved of a settlement, precluding the need for a trial. He had also stayed in his office late on Friday and Saturday as well, and deliberately left his house telephone number, expecting to hear from either side. But no one called. The trial was set for Monday morning at nine o'clock.

On Monday morning, Mike stood before the six jurors and six alternates. He wore his blue suit, the same one he had worn on his last court victory in a malpractice suit nearly two years earlier. It was not uncommon for personal injury plaintiff attorneys to hardly ever go to trial. Most cases were settled close to a trial date to avoid the high costs associated with trial work and to lock in settlement amounts for clients with questionable claims. He faced the jurors, arms folded, and gave them his most serious face.

This was Mike's opportunity to pour it on, to really showcase the strength of his claims right from the outset. There were about one hundred spectators in the courtroom, all seated. Judge Cromwell had been specific. "If you can't find a seat, you will have to leave."

Mike was tired. He had been up most of the weekend as he continuously rehearsed his speech. He had instructed the family members of the victims not to attend the trial unless they were summoned to do so. Any sign of emotion by them at the wrong time might not sit well with the jurors.

After a long pause, which to some in the courtroom appeared to last forever, Mike took a deep breath and walked directly in front of the jurors.

"Ladies and gentlemen of the jury," he began. "There is a huge condominium development in North Smithfield where hundreds of units were built for people seeking an alternate lifestyle from owning single-family homes. These units were constructed between 1980 and 1983 by a contractor who deliberately avoided action which would have protected the unit owners from a health hazard that spread in the ground under the condominium complex it was built on. This hazard is called radon gas, and we will show you how overexposure to radon gas over a period of time resulted in twelve owners getting lung cancer and subsequently dying from it."

He told the jury about the twelve victims living in condo units in the complex, and not a single one a smoker. He would prove, he said, the building contractor deliberately falsified engineering reports that warned of this potential hazard for the sake of saving money by not having to take corrective action. The contractor, he continued, did not let any buyers know that the potential for radon existed, which would have at least given these people the opportunity to take their own corrective action. "The contractor simply did not care; even though he knew what he hid from them could seriously hurt them or lead to death."

When Mike was done, you could hear a pin drop in the courtroom. It was as if the spectators were in a trance. Judge Cromwell broke the silence as he called for a brief recess before Kubaska gave his opening statement. The defense lawyers were stunned by Mike's opening comments, essentially calling Tate Builders murderers to save a few bucks. Kubaska also noticed the jurors' reaction to the effects of radon gas in homes. He believed this was possibly the first time many jurors ever heard about radon. He worried that many of them, when not sitting on the jury, would now consider having radon tests in their own homes. To Kubaska, this would be trouble if Mike could convince them of the danger of the gas, especially due to the failure to inform owners of its existence.

As the jurors were reseated following the recess, Kubaska himself rose for the defense's opening statement. He had decided to do the opening because he was much older than his younger associates and the jury might warm up to him more. The younger attorneys might appear too aggressive and indifferent in their presentation to a jury comprised mostly of older people.

"Ladies and gentlemen of the jury, my name is Rupert Kubaska, and I would like to tell you a story," he began.

"In December 1984, Stanley Watras accidentally set off a radiation detection device when he reported to work. Watras triggered the alarm while approximately three feet away from a radiation detection device at the Limerick Nuclear Power Plant where he worked as an engineer. After it was determined that Watras was not picking up radiation at the power plant, Watras and his wife decided to test their split level home in Boyertown, Pennsylvania. They discovered that their home was contaminated with an excess amount of radon. The home registered a reading of forty-four hundred picocuries per liter of air, more than one thousand times the EPA's suggested minimum of four picocuries. The radon levels in the home were said to be the equivalent of smoking one hundred thirty five packs of cigarettes per day," he continued. Mike wondered where this was leading.

"What made the Watras case so noteworthy and news-worthy was the distressing fact that the extremely high radon levels were the result of an entirely natural phe-nomenon. The Watras' lived in an efficiently constructed home, relatively airtight. As Stanley Watras stated, 'Man didn't put radon in the ground, who are we going to sue, God?' Naturally occurring residential radon comes from uranium in the earth's crust. Virtually every geographic area contains some amount, but higher radon gas levels are more highly concentrated, especially in New England," Kubaska went on. He had the jury's full attention.

"Radon gas enters houses and builds to high concentrations in many ways. Usually, radon gas seeps through cracks in foundations and tiny pores or cracks in hollow-block walls. It can also come through openings made specifically for sewer, water or gas line pipes. You cannot totally prevent radon gas seepage, and it is impossible to build a home, or condominium complex, which prevents the entry of radon gas. My client was not negligent when he omitted telling buyers there might be radon on the property. State law does not require investigation of the property to determine whether a condition exists. We will show, without a doubt, there was no negligence by our client. The implied warranty of habitability holds that a builder warrants a home is built in a workmanlike manner and is reasonably fit for the purpose for which it is sold."

Kubaska had said everything he intended to say. Not accustomed to speaking often before a jury, he was satisfied with the hour long presentation as he returned to his seat at the defense table.

Mike was prepared to call as many as ten witnesses in the radon phase of the trial. He knew how important it was for the jury to agree to contractor negligence in order for him to get to the medical phase where damages would be sought. He would rely mainly on the testimony of two witnesses. The first one was Rocco Santini, the owner of Siteco Engineering and, ironically, the brother-in-law of Jonathan Tate, the lead defendant in the case. Mike expected Santini to verify his signature on the engineering report prepared by his company. The second witness was even bigger. Mike had agreed to pay for all the expenses of a senior executive with the assistant surgeon general's office from the U.S. Public Health Service to speak on the hazards of radon exposure. This testimony would make the jury aware of the national attention radon gas exposure captured.

While Santini's testimony might be considered hostile, Mike believed he would not lie under oath. He was merely attesting to his signature on a report he always signed at the end of his company's engagement. Phil McKenna, the D.C. aide, on the other hand, needed coaching. Mike had asked him, "They're going to ask, 'Are you being paid for your testimony?' What do you think you should answer?" The senior executive hesitated. "Yes...?" he answered weakly.

"No, no, no! You are being *compensated* for your time. And, please, wear a very conservative suit and tie."

Mike's plan was to continuously keep the momentum in his favor by calling witness after witness to testify on the cancer-causing effects of radon if left unchecked. Rupert's strategy was to constantly object to these witnesses' testimony as being hearsay and unproven. Rupert's main objection was to get the engineering report thrown out because the evidence was not obtained with permission from the engineering company. Mike would not reveal how he obtained this report because he had promised Rudy Dionne from Siteco he would not put him at risk with his company when he provided Ralph with the complete report.

Mike called Santini to the stand. He approached him with a two-hundred page document dated August 13, 1979, entitled *Engineering Report for Rock Ridge Common*. He asked Santini to flip through the report to the last page.

"Mr. Santini, is this your signature on the report?" Mike asked the witness as he pointed to the name at the bottom of the page.

"Yes, it is," Santini answered.

"Were you ever asked to change this report at any time after discussing its contents with your client, Tate Builders?"

"No, sir. To my knowledge, this is the only report we prepared back then," Santini replied.

"Mr. Santini, what is your relationship with the defendant, other than as your one-time client?" Mike asked. He noticed Kubaska at the edge of his seat, ready to jump in and protest.

"Objection, Your Honor, relevance?"

"Your Honor, I'm trying to point out to the jury that if there was a reason for Siteco to alter the contents of their report, such a change might occur as a result of the client's relationship with the company or the principals in the company."

"Overruled," Judge Cromwell replied. "The witness will answer the question." Kubaska was not pleased.

"Jonathan Tate is my brother-in-law, my wife's brother."

"So, Mr. Santini, is it safe to say that if this report were to be changed by you or someone else in your company, your relationship with the defendant might have something to do with this?"

"Mr. Strange, Siteco Engineering doesn't operate this way. We do not haphazardly change reports merely to accommodate a client, even if the client is my brother-in-law."

"So, you would state here, without any doubt, this is the only report you sent to Tate Builders with your conclusions regarding the site in question?' Mike emphasized.

"Because of our relationship, I personally oversaw this project and do not ever remember another report being sent to Mr. Tate."

Mike returned to the plaintiffs' table, retrieved a second document, and presented it to Santini.

"Mr. Santini, please turn to page fifty-one of this report." Mike then opened the first document to the same page.

"Do you see a difference in the section entitled *Environmental and Hazardous Material* from both reports?"

"Why, yes, there is a whole section missing in this report from the first one."

Mike asked Santini to read the section mentioning the prevalence of radon on the site from the first document, and asked him, in his opinion, why the section was omitted from the second report. Santini shook his head to indicate he did not know.

"Are you aware the second document without the radon disclosure is the report on file in North Smithfield?" Mike asked.

"Filing a report with the town is the contractor's responsibility, not ours. I am not aware which of these documents was filed with the town."

"No further questions, Your Honor."

"Mr. Kubaska, do you wish to cross examine this witness?" Judge Cromwell asked.

Kubaska jumped to his feet and walked directly in front of Santini on the witness stand.

"Mr. Santini, how would you describe your relationship with Mr. Tate?"

"It was fine. This was Jonathan's first big project, so there was a learning curve on his part, but we got through it fine."

"How do you know which of these two reports is the real one?"

"If there had been a second report to remove or add information to the original report, my signature on the second report would have a small circled number two next to it. This way, I always know which report came first, especially when the date on each report is the same. Both of these reports do not have the number two next to my name, which likely means one of these reports was doctored."

"How is it you believe the one filed in the town is the one which was changed?" Kubaska asked.

"Because I brought the original file with me which has the original signatures from our company, and the section in question is much more detailed than this one filed in North Smithfield."

Kubaska's mouth dropped open. He had not expected Santini to volunteer this information. It seemed that Rudy Dionne's comment to Ralph Pennington months earlier held true to form. Siteco would not falsify a report, not even for a brother-in-law.

CHAPTER 22

On Tuesday morning, following what Mike considered was an excellent first day of the trial, he called his next witness to the stand.

"Would you please state your name and occupation for the court, please?" Mike asked.

"My name is Tom Brisson, presently retired, but formerly the building inspector for the Town of North Smithfield and a member of the planning board."

"Mr. Brisson, were you the building inspector and on the planning board in 1979 when the Rock Ridge Common condominium project was proposed?"

"Yes, I was."

"And, in your capacity, did you have access to and review the engineering report filed with the town for that project?"

"Of course. It was our responsibility to make sure there were no reasons to prevent such a project from going forward. The site engineers' report is a vital piece of the process," Brisson answered.

"So, let me be perfectly clear here. If there was information in the engineering report which required follow-up action, the town would only issue permits subject to the necessary corrections to be made by the contractor. Is that fair to say?"

"Objection, Your Honor," Kubaska yelled. "The question begs for an opinion only, and one from a person long since removed from the process."

"Your Honor, the witness' opinion is based on twenty years on the job in North Smithfield, having dealt with many similar projects where engineering reports needed to be reviewed. I believe Mr. Brisson is qualified to answer this question," Mike rebutted.

"I agree, counsel. Objection is overruled," Judge Cromwell stated.

"Because the town is small, we don't employ full-time engineers who can review site reports in detail. We rely on people in the building trades who sit on the planning board and can understand what's in the engineering reports, like the one from Siteco. If there was anything questionable on the piece of property which needed to be addressed, then we would insist on corrective action before allowing the project to move forward," Brisson answered.

Mike reached for the report filed with the town and showed it to Brisson.

"Is this the report reviewed by you and other members of the planning board on the Rock Ridge Common project?"

"Yes, it is. You can see the stamp from the planning department on the last page of the document, August 16, 1979, with my initials."

"Now, let me show you the actual report the town should have received and reviewed. In an effort to save the court some time, Your Honor, I have highlighted only the part of the report which was omitted from the town's copy. Would you read that part for the court, Mr. Brisson?"

As Brisson read the section on *Environmental and Health Hazards* from the original report, his face clearly began to show signs of anger. He could not believe what he was reading. He suddenly blurted loudly, "Are you kidding me?" Kubaska could see the jury listening very carefully and, again, he was not pleased.

"Is there a problem, in your opinion, Mr. Brisson, with what's in this section?" asked Mike as he faced the jury. He stayed focused on them as Brisson answered.

"There is no way in hell the town would have allowed building permits to be issued without a detailed plan from the contractor on how this situation would be corrected, no way. And I can come up with dozens of similar environmental and health issues from other plans which were treated in the same way. The town would never have allowed this project to go forward had we read this report. This was not a difficult issue to resolve. All they would have had to do was seal the floors and walls in the basements."

"No further questions, Your Honor."

Kubaska had nothing he could argue against. This engineering report turned out to be a bigger thorn than he imagined. He bit his lip as he stated to the judge, "No questions at this time, Your Honor."

"Before I move on to my next witness, Your Honor, I would like to point out to the court and the jury certain facts. In Lingsch v. Savage in 1963, it clearly states that *where the seller knows facts materially affecting the value or desirability of the property and the facts are only accessible to him, and where the facts are not known to or within the reach of the buyer, the seller is under the duty to disclose.* Clearly, the builder who is aware of a radon condition on the property, or in the home, is under a duty to disclose this information to the potential buyer."

Judge Cromwell jotted down the date and case cited by Mike to the jurors and then told him to move on. Several other witnesses were called to express their view on whether they would have bought a condo unit at Rock Ridge had they known ahead of time there was radon on the grounds the condos sat on. Kubaska countered each of these witnesses by producing a copy of their purchase agreement. On page eighteen of the agreement, in small print, was a statement that read, "Buyer is free to conduct radon tests of the unit prior to sale. Owner makes no determination one way or another as to the presence of radon gas on the property." Mike rebutted this language as being vague and buried in small print, following page after page of clauses a normal buyer would never read, nor likely understand. Judge Cromwell, nonetheless, expressed that such language did exist in the purchase agreement. Mike decided not to pursue this course because he felt jurors would relate in his favor at the frustration of items in small print in documents.

Dr. Phil McKenna would be Mike's last witness in this phase of the trial. Mike kept his fingers crossed on his upcoming testimony. If all went well, he thought he had submitted enough proof to enable the jury to allow the trial to move to the medical damages phase. Dr. McKenna, a senior executive to Dr. Henry Vernon, Assistant Surgeon General of the U.S. Public Health Service, was no stranger to public speaking. He was the in-house spokesperson for the agency that made numerous public appearances at medical conventions and seminars, discussing various medical issues of interest including, of late, the hazards of radon exposure. Mike had coached McKenna on what to say and what not to say. It was important to his case to leave the jury with the impression radon gas was now a national issue of concern. McKenna agreed to be brief in his answers when questioned, but convincing.

"Dr. McKenna, in your role at the U.S. Public Health Service, has radon gas ever been discussed?"

"Discussed, not only has it been discussed, sir, it is one of the hottest medical issues most people know very little about," McKenna replied.

"Can you be more specific, Doctor?"

"For years, people were of the impression that because radon gas was colorless and odorless, it was harmless. If you can't smell it or see it, how can it be so bad? So, people ignored its existence. A reporter from the *Philadelphia Inquirer* last year did a great story on the subject. He claimed radon causes nearly twenty thousand deaths each year from lung cancer. As a result of this information, federal officials issued a national health advisory warning that millions of homes have elevated radon levels."

"Basically, Doctor, what dangers does the U.S. Public Health Service find in exposure to high levels of radon?" Mike queried.

"Well, my boss, the assistant surgeon general, said radon exceeds by ten times the threat posed by outdoor air pollution. Radon exposure raises the risk of lung cancer for a nonsmoker to that of a smoker. He would not buy a home, nor move into a home, without knowing what the radon content is in it. Ironically, the situation can be easily minimized."

"What do you mean by that?"

"In September, 1987, there were guidelines issued by the National Association of Homebuilders to its builders for radon-reduced construction. Although builders are not required to build homes free of radon, these guidelines provide techniques with which to construct houses with seals and ventilation in the right places."

"But the builder has to be willing to follow these guidelines rather than avoid them. Is that correct, Doctor?"

"Objection, Your Honor, the good doctor, last I checked, is not a builder. How builders interpret guidelines is out of his element," Kubaska claimed.

"Sustained. You are not to answer, Dr. McKenna," Judge Cromwell stated.

"One more question, Dr. McKenna. In your opinion, what would you say are the odds of twelve people dying from lung cancer in a five-year period, all from the same residential area?"

"Objection. Speculative," Kubaska rose again.

"Sustained. Would you like to rephrase your question, Mr. Strange?" Judge Cromwell asked.

"Yes, Your Honor. Dr. McKenna, have there been studies done on the effects of overexposure to radon gas?"

"As far back as 1972, there was a study by the National Academy of Sciences Committee on the Biological Effects of Ionizing Radiation. They found the incidence of cancer among American workers was directly proportional to their exposure to radon gas."

As Mike sat down and Rupert rose to cross examine Dr. McKenna, he could see the concern on the faces of the jurors. In Mike's mind, he knew the information was eye opening to most of them. There would likely be several radon tests performed in the coming weeks.

"Dr. McKenna," Kubaska began, "how long does a person need to be exposed to high radon levels before he potentially can develop lung cancer?"

"This is a difficult question to answer. In some cases, it might be five years, in others as much as twenty years. There are other factors to consider such as the level of picocuries on the premises, the existing health of the individual, and the frequency of exposure to radon gas."

"So, would it be a fair statement to say that no one case is alike, some five years, but some twenty years or more. And some not at all, is that correct?"

"Yes, that is correct."

"What would you then say the odds would be of twelve people in the same complex all dying from lung cancer within five years?"

"Objection, Your Honor, speculation," Mike shouted.

"I'll sustain the objection, Mr. Strange, but the both of you are trying my patience with this line of questioning," Judge Cromwell growled.

"No further questions, Your Honor."

Mike knew the last discussion would raise some doubt with jurors on radon causing the deaths of all twelve people in such a short period of time. Nonetheless, he thought they would consider the likelihood of at least some of the victims having developed fatal lung cancer because of radon exposure, some of them exposed for up to ten years. He had no more witnesses and it was now time for Kubaska to begin his side of the issues.

It had taken nearly a week for all of Mike's witnesses to testify, and Judge Cromwell asked Kubaska if he was ready with his witnesses for the next day. Kubaska indicated he did not need more time and would call his first witness the next morning.

Mike was not ready to go back to his office after a long day at court. He called Bonnie at home and asked if she would like company for dinner. He offered to bring Chinese from the local restaurant near her condominium building in Lincoln, along with a bottle of wine. Bonnie thought the break from trial would be good for him and, besides, she loved being with him. Mike could unwind with an early dinner before he headed back to his office to review Kubaska's witness list.

Momentum. I must keep up the momentum, he thought.

CHAPTER 23

Kubaska and his associates from Mutual of New England called their first witness on Friday morning, Arnold Dale from the Environmental Protection Agency.

"Mr. Dale," Kubaska began. "If given the present knowledge of the radon problem, a reasonable builder did not use certain building methods or materials when constructing a home in a radon-prone area, could this be seen as a breach of workmanlike construction?"

"Yes and no. It depends on the jurisdiction. Some courts hold that a warranty guarantees the home will have no defects which substantially impair the enjoyment of the home. Other courts apply the warranty only when the home is virtually uninhabitable."

"Did your group inspect the property at Rock Ridge at the outset of the project?"

"We did, and even if there were traces of radon on the property, at this time there is no direct regulation forcing a builder to address the problem. It is possible for a house to become contaminated with radon using state-of-the-art construction without any design or manufacturing defect. To my knowledge, from a construction point of view, the units at Rock Ridge were well-built."

"No further questions, Your Honor."

"Mr. Strange, do you have questions for this witness?" Judge Cromwell asked.

"Yes, Your Honor. Mr. Dale, in your opinion, do you believe the defendants had a moral obligation to reveal the likelihood of radon on the property in question?"

"Not if they intended to take care of the issue. On the other hand, if the builder deliberately took no action after radon tests came in at high levels, then one could wonder why no follow-up occurred. In this case, to my knowledge, no radon tests were performed by the builders and they were under no obligation to perform such tests, since the engineering report only suggested the presence of radon, not the level."

"In other words, sir," added Mike, "because the defendants were not aware of radon in any specific units, since they never tested any of them, they had no information to reveal to owners, even if there was a likelihood of radon existing in some units according to the engineers' report?"

"Basically, that's the way it is today. The laws right now do not require contractors to test all homes they build for radon, even if site reports suggest there is radon on the property. It remains the responsibility of each homeowner right now, or in this case, of each condo owner."

When the witness was excused, Mike felt a lump in his throat. These statements didn't help the plaintiffs in attempts to show negligence. Hopefully, he would fare better with other witnesses for the defense.

Kubaska now called David Knollwood, an environmental lawyer from the firm of Brock, Penner and Knollwood from Boston.

"Mr. Knollwood, as an expert in environmental law, can you explain to the court about radon gas, and the contingency to a building contractor as it exists today?"

"Certainly. When a contractor knows for sure the level of radon exposure in a home or on a piece of property where the homes will be built, he is under a moral obligation to remedy the situation or at least offer some sort of credit off the purchase price, and the owner is responsible to remedy the exposure. If the level of radon is not defined enough for the contractor to know if the level may exceed EPA-accepted levels, then the obligation to reveal is vaguer. Quite honestly, the detection of radon has caused few real estate deals to fall through, even though prolonged exposure to high concentrations of the gas is believed to cause cancer."

"Why, in your opinion, Mr. Knollwood, considering radon contamination in the home is claimed to cause significant life-threatening risks, hasn't there been greater evidence of public concern through litigation on the issue?" Kubaska asked.

"To be perfectly honest, the latency period of up to twenty years or more for the development of radon-induced lung cancer is an impediment to plaintiffs in suing for damages in radon litigation. The lack of public interest on the issue, in my opinion, is the main reason you haven't seen many cases on the subject."

"And, in your opinion, what is the reason for such lack of interest in radon cases?"

"Clearly, the EPA has to take much of the blame. The EPA has taken a very simplistic, arbitrary approach in testing and mitigation. They underestimated the number of deaths likely attributable to lung cancer from radon exposure and failed miserably to alert the public on varying levels of radon from one home to another. Let me give you an example. One of your neighbors tests for radon and gets a low reading. The rest of the neighborhood now believes no radon exists, so the neighbors don't bother with their own test. If someone gets a high reading, the others don't want to hear about it. The public is, and remains, simply confused about the dangers of radon."

"I have no further questions for this witness, Your Honor."

Mike rose to his feet and approached Knollwood in a rage. "Are you telling the court that the builder has no obligation nor suffers any consequences at knowing the existence of radon on a property, and deliberately avoiding revealing such existence to buyers?"

"Yes, that's exactly what I'm saying. Apathy is the most significant reason this is still not addressed. People relate lung cancer to smoking or asbestos or lead poisoning, not to radon. Most people have never heard of radon tests in homes. The gas is colorless, odorless, and tasteless-so it is out of sight, out of mind. The contractor is not the villain here. He did not put the radon there. It is a national risk which people underestimate and ignore."

"But, Mr. Knollwood, why would a contractor deliberately remove clauses about radon existence if he wasn't trying to hide the danger?" Mike asked.

"Objection, Your Honor, speculation. Mr. Knollwood is not a mind reader," Kubaska blared.

"Sustained. Rephrase, Mr. Strange?"

"So, you would state, Mr. Knollwood, the blame here belongs to all of us?"

"People, who choose their homes, voluntarily expose themselves to radon, and, before 1986, information about radon to consider when choosing homes was hard to obtain. And there is no obvious perceptual link between exposure and death."

"Objection. Witness is not a medical expert, Your Honor," Mike explained.

"Sustained."

"What I'm trying to state is that the public simply does not take the indoor radon threat seriously. This is the fault of our government's passive approach to the issue in the last ten years. If radon truly is a life-threatening issue as it appears to be, based on scientific evidence, then new approaches to reach the public about the seriousness of the radon problem must be proposed, examined, and implemented."

Once Mike had completed his questions to Knollwood, he wasn't sure if the jury tended to absolve Tate Builders of any guilt, or if he himself believed more should have been done by the individual victims to mitigate the radon in their units. Other owners after them were now testing as more awareness to the problem arose.

The defense rested.

CHAPTER 24

On the day following the final arguments, Judge Cromwell instructed the jurors on the rules of law they were to follow to reach a verdict. This took about an hour. He then excused the six alternate jurors in the case for the time being, reminding them they were still jurors in the case and could not discuss their views with anyone. The six regular jurors then went off to begin their deliberations.

Following the judge's instructions to the jury, the courtroom emptied quickly, with no one really aware of how long their deliberations would take. A federal marshal was assigned to guard the closed door to the jury room.

Mike went back to his office to wait for news from the jurors. The following morning, he arrived in the corridor of the jury room before eight o'clock, when the jurors would arrive, and left to go back to his office a few hours later.

The wait was agonizing to Mike. Kubaska had returned to Boston and would only appear in court when a decision had been made. To just hang around a Providence courtroom was below his dignity and he would not be seen in those circumstances by his associates.

Three days passed and still no decision. Each morning, Mike would return to the courthouse and ask, "Any word?"

"Nothing yet," the marshal outside the jury room would indicate to Mike. "Someone will call your office as soon as they're out."

"I know, I know. I just didn't expect it to take so long."

Finally, on the fourth day, at eleven in the morning, the jury had reached a verdict. News carried quickly and court would be in session at two in the afternoon. A crowd of spectators and journalists began to assemble in the corridor shortly after one, Mike with his hands clasped in prayer and focusing on the hardwood floor in the courtroom.

At five minutes before two, the jurors filed down and took their seats in the courtroom. Judge Cromwell's clerk asked the foreman to rise.

"Mr. Foreman, members of the jury, have you agreed on a verdict?"

"Yes, we have," replied the foreman, who handed the jury slip to the clerk.

The judge unfolded the slip and read in silence. Then in a formal voice, he announced:

"With respect to the issue of negligence on the part of the defendants, they have answered 'yes' to willful neglect in the lack of disclosure of radon on the property in question."

When the judge finished reading the jury's answers, he said, "These answers now require that we proceed to the second stage of the trial. I will meet with counsel to determine the date when this phase will begin."

He told the lawyers he would spend the month of January in Florida. "I'd like to look at your briefs in early February when I get back. If there's going to be further trial of the case, which it certainly appears there will be unless a settlement is reached, I propose to start on Monday, February nineteenth."

The judge excused the jury until that date but reminded them, "The case is still going on," he said. "We'll take a small break for the holidays, and meet again on the nineteenth. Enjoy the holidays."

Mike called Bonnie at home. He told her about the verdict and asked her to notify the twelve plaintiffs. He wanted them to meet as a group at his office the following day.

Kubaska was surrounded by reporters and microphones as he was bombarded with questions on the outcome. All he could reply was, "After the holidays, we are looking forward to the second phase of the case."

Mike also was overwhelmed by microphones as he stood on the courthouse steps, bundled with his winter coat and scarf on a chilly November afternoon.

"To expect homeowners to know or understand the meaning of items in small print on documents and expect them to address radon is troubling. Most people will not do this if they do not understand the health effects of exposure and the fact that a test is required to know the levels in a particular home. The defendants chose to ignore the potential health hazard and this is unacceptable. At a minimum, as more knowledge about radon and its effects grows, the builders of homes in radon-prone areas must be expected both to determine if a radon problem exists, and to disclose the problem to buyers. This was a senseless way to lose loved ones. These losses could have been avoided."

* * *

"Are you up to venturing out early tonight?" Mike asked Bonnie on the other end of the phone. "I can be there by five, and help you get in my car. We can have a nice quiet celebration at the Mill House Restaurant. We haven't won yet, but it looks promising we may be able to settle before we have to go back to trial in February. If you're not up to it, maybe I can pick up something for your place."

"Well, Mr. Big Winner, I guess I've got to go out some-time and I'm getting a serious case of cabin fever anyway. Tonight sounds as good as any to make my debut back to civilization. I can be ready by five," Bonnie answered. "By the way, all but Mrs. Collamati can make it to your office tomorrow at two. She's got the flu, and with Thanksgiving right around the corner, she's trying to shake it. Apparently, she still does the cooking for the rest of the family. But she wanted me to thank you for now. She'll do the honors her-self next week, hopefully."

"Great, see you then."

Mike then called Diane at the Mill House Restaurant. He asked her if there was a very quiet corner where he could bring Bonnie for dinner. He explained to Diane how she was still showing the effects of bruises and cuts on her arms and face, and that her walk was very shaky. Diane told Mike, if she had a wheelchair, she could come through the side entrance by using the ramp on this side. Dinner was set for five forty-five.

He arrived at Bonnie's condo at four forty-five and Bonnie wasn't quite ready yet. She had poured them each a glass of chardonnay sitting on the kitchen counter. She yelled from the bedroom for him to help himself as she would be out shortly.

Mike picked up his glass and took a generous sip. The chilled wine was refreshing after a hectic day in court, and dealing with the press afterwards. Mike was still on his feet moments later when Bonnie appeared. As Mike turned to greet her, his mouth dropped and he nearly dropped his wine glass.

"Wow, you look great, wow," he fumbled for words.

Bonnie's brown hair, normally tied back in a pony-tail, was loose and flowed over her shoulders. Her hair was perfectly groomed. But what attracted Mike most was the gleam in her eyes and the wonderful job she had done covering most of the facial cuts and bruises. She wore dark slacks with a matching blouse, covered perfectly by a beautiful blazer which covered all the bruises and Band-Aids still on her arms. You would never have known she had been in a near fatal crash just a few months earlier.

She slowly walked toward Mike, being careful not to limp or buckle on the way. To Mike's surprise, she kissed him hard on the lips, and then pulled back.

"That's from Mrs. Collamati. She told me to give you a big kiss from her, so I did."

"Well, did anyone else tell you to thank me on their behalf?" he smiled as he handed her the other wine glass from the counter.

"Here's to your quick full recovery, although it sure looks to me like you're almost there. And here's to our biggest victory so far and, hopefully, a settlement offer before February nineteenth."

They clanked glasses and enjoyed the moment. *This girl won't need a wheelchair tonight,* he pondered. In a short while, they were off to the Mill House where dinner was perfect. Bonnie had not been to a restaurant in over two months and she especially enjoyed being there with Mike. Time seemed to fly as neither cared about anything else but enjoying the moment. They were both quiet on the drive back to Lincoln, and as Mike pulled up to Bonnie's condo, he leaned over to give Bonnie a harmless kiss goodnight.

"Thank you for celebrating with me. There would have been only one other person I would have done this with a short while ago. You've become someone special to me, Bonnie. Have a good night. We'll talk soon."

Bonnie beamed a smile she had been saving all night long, and she walked slowly back to the front door of her condo. She wanted to do this by herself. She was determined to be back to normal and in the office again soon, assuming she was no longer in danger.

Time would tell.

CHAPTER 25

Thanksgiving to Mike was a non-event. Susan and he had spent most of the day a year ago at Susan's parents. Alice loved cooking, and Susan and her mother would spend hours in the kitchen chatting about anything and everything as much as preparing the traditional holiday dinner. Even with the recent favorable court decision, Mike was in no mood for a family dinner. Thoughts of Susan's death ran through his mind and he wanted to be alone. Ralph and Alice understood his decision, and hoped he would try to rest over the weekend.

On the Friday after the holiday, he went to his office in Providence. The office gave him a sense of security. He immersed himself into several other cases his associate had been working on, and realized how far behind he was as a result of all the attention the trial had required. A call to Sergeant Lemoine in Cumberland resulted in the same reply as the five previous calls.

"Mr. Strange, I'm sorry to say we have nothing new to report on your wife's murder. It appears we've reached a dead end on the case. No one has yet to come forward who saw anything on the day of your wife's murder, other than the Venture cable truck out front. When we recovered the stolen truck, there were no prints, no cigarette butts or empty cups, nothing."

The solitude in the office was deafening. He found his mind constantly wandering away from the very cases he tried to review. He kept thinking about who would do such a heinous thing to Susan, and he started sobbing as he often did when he was alone at night at home.

Suddenly, there stood Bonnie in the outer doorway. She wore a pair of blue slacks and a navy colored sweater under a brown blazer, and she used a cane to help her regain her balance as she walked in. Mike quickly wiped the tears from his eyes as she pushed the door to his private office wide open.

"I knew I'd find you here. I'm back, and I need to catch up on some cases. Do you mind the company?" she asked.

"Heck no, Bonnie, but are you sure you're up to it?"

"We'll soon find out, won't we? Anything I can do on the radon case?"

"I'm hoping we can work out some settlement before February nineteenth. Even though Tate should have told people about the radon, I'm not sure I can prove that all twelve people died from radon exposure. Everything I read tells me radon takes a long time before it can turn into lung cancer, longer than the ten years the condos have been up. I might have a better chance with the victims who had been there from the beginning in 1979 or 1980. But all of them, I doubt it. It all depends how much Mutual is willing to offer to avoid another trial. They know juries tend to be sympathetic to victims when you're dealing with insurance company money. Tate originally wanted to offer them over six million to avoid going to court. If Kubaska was in that ballpark, I'd recommend to our clients to settle."

"I'm kind of new at this settlement negotiation stuff, Mike. Who makes the first move, you or Kubaska?"

"Normally, the defendant makes the first move, but doesn't do it too quickly. Kubaska doesn't appear to be the type of guy who wants to concede anything right now. But maybe once we get into late January, he might throw a bone our way. It could be interesting after we toss out what I expect to be a very low settlement offer."

"Sounds to me like a poker game. Who's bluffing, and who's for real. Question is, who's going to fold first?" Bonnie added.

"I've got to catch up on all these other cases first. Do you have work on some cases you can catch up on?" Mike asked as he buried his face in the piles of documents in front of him.

"I'll be at my desk and see if I can get back up to speed myself. Give me a shout if you need anything."

Bonnie had clearly caught the tears in Mike's eyes when she entered his office, even though she immediately turned the other way from Mike at that moment. She could feel the pain he was going through at this time of year. What should have been festive moments in his life, had become an overnight nightmare. Her sorrow for his anguish built up inside of her as she could feel her own tears taking over. Bonnie adored this man, the only person she felt sexually attracted to. She had felt this way from the first day he had agreed to represent her in her liability suit from the auto accident years earlier. Later, when she became his secretary, she did all she could to suppress her feelings for him, envying his wife Susan for having made such a terrific catch. Now, months after his wife's murder, she hoped to one day be more than just a paralegal to Mike. But she could see he was not ready for another relationship at the moment. She would wait. *Good things come to those who are patient,* she pondered.

Both of them worked in separate offices for hours, neither taking time for lunch. At four o'clock, Mike emerged from his office and seemed more cheerful.

"I've had enough of this stuff for one day. Want to stop at Capriccio's for a cocktail, and maybe an early dinner?"

"I sort of have my second wind right now, Mike, and I think I'll stay a while longer. But thanks for the offer," she replied.

"Well, if you change your mind, I'll be the good-looking guy sitting at the bar," he added.

No sooner than Mike had left, Bonnie felt her heart beating very fast. She wanted to go with him, but something inside of her told her to move more slowly with him. She was not looking for just a quick moment with Mike on the rebound. She wanted him to come to her ready for a lasting relationship, not a one-night stand. Not that all her suitors were standing in line to have sex with her, Bonnie had hardly ever thought about what she wanted in a man. Her bruises and ailments were not attractive characteristics, and her lack of social graces was evident. She rarely dated, and when she did, a second date almost never happened. She didn't care. For now, working with Mike was enough to satisfy her appetite for men.

Two hours later, Bonnie started to get tired. Perhaps she had overdone her first day back to work. Providence on the day after Thanksgiving is virtually a ghost town. Most restaurants in the downtown area are either closed or open until eight o'clock. The city was not a destination stop for non-business dining, and many eateries would not survive without the business lunches and dinners geared for executives in the capital city.

As Bonnie wrapped up her work and locked the office door behind her, she decided to drive the short distance to Capriccio's, and celebrate her return to work. The restaurant had valet parking, so she wouldn't need to walk too far on her still-recuperating legs. She was convinced Mike would no longer be there at this time as she entered the restaurant and descended the staircase to the shiny cobblestone floor on the lower level. The maître'd welcomed her and escorted her to a quiet table along the wall.

"So, you're avoiding me, aren't you?" came a voice from the adjoining bar area.

"Mike, you're still here. I thought for certain you'd already left by now. And, no, I'm not trying to avoid you. But I think you need your own space right now."

"Actually, I decided to walk over here because I needed the cool fresh air, and I bumped into an old law school buddy from Northeastern. We chatted for about an hour over a cup of coffee at the Weybosset Diner. I invited him here for a drink, but come to find out, he doesn't drink. Can you imagine a lawyer who doesn't drink? So, I've only been here for a little more than a half hour and I'm still on my first martini. And, if you don't mind being in my space right now, I'd still like to have dinner with you. May I join you?"

Mike reached down and kissed her on the cheek as he sat down next to her. He ordered another martini and a glass of chardonnay for Bonnie. The next few hours flew by as Mike seemed more talkative than ever. Perhaps the martinis made him feel more at ease. They ate dinner in a relatively quiet and somewhat empty dining area. Capriccio's stopped serving dinner at eight, and most customers had already left. When Mike paid the tab, the waiter signaled to the maître'd to have the valet bring her car out front. The insurance company had totaled her rental car after the crash in Slatersville, but her own car had been repaired while she recuperated at home. Mike gave Bonnie another kiss on the cheek and decided to walk back to his office on Weybosset Street, just a short distance away. She told him she would likely be in the office again either on Saturday or Sunday.

He went back to the office and tried to focus on more legal issues, but found himself distracted by thoughts of Bonnie. He had never thought of her in an intimate way before, but he suddenly realized how attractive she was to him. In the next few minutes, he locked his office, walked to his car in the adjacent lot, and picked up Route 146 on his way toward home in Cumberland. He turned off on Route 116 and stopped at the traffic light facing the Lincoln High School. As if by impulse, when the light turned green, he took a left toward the Kirkbrae Apartments where Bonnie lived. He couldn't stop himself as his car pulled up in front of her apartment at nine o'clock. He could see the lights still on through her apartment windows and rang the doorbell. A few seconds went by and the front door opened.

Bonnie stood there in her bathrobe and didn't know what to say as she gazed at Mike. He entered the doorway, shut the door, and grabbed Bonnie by the waist and drew her to him.

"I don't want to be alone tonight. I don't like being alone, Bonnie," he said as he held her tightly and began to kiss her over and over.

"Those were for the other clients who wanted to thank me the other day and couldn't make the meeting," he whispered as he kissed her again and again.

"Are you sure you want to do this, Mike?" she asked as she gently touched his face with one hand.

"I've never been more certain of anything than right now."

She helped him remove his jacket, and started to untie his shirt as he quickly tossed it aside. He reached for the sash holding her bathrobe closed, and pulled the robe open. His eyes suddenly focused on her totally naked body beneath the robe.

"So much for taking my clothes off, right?" she said as she reached for the belt on his pants. She led him to her bedroom across the living room area, and threw herself on the bed, tossing her robe away.

Mike removed his pants and quickly was on top of her. Neither of them wanted to stop, until finally, Mike fell to Bonnie's side staring at the ceiling.

"I'm so sorry, Bonnie. I shouldn't have come here tonight."

"Was I a disappointment to you, Mike, or do you feel sorry for taking advantage of me?" she asked.

"Oh, no, it's not you. Oh my God, you were wonderful. I'm going through a tough time these days and I really wanted to be with you. I don't know where this is going, but I'd like to find out."

"You don't have to leave, you know. Stay the night and leave in the morning. I make a mean omelet."

Mike looked at Bonnie and could easily notice the warmth in her eyes and the gentleness of her touch. He turned to kiss her again, and one thing led to another, until they both fell sound asleep. When Bonnie awoke the next morning, Mike was gone. Their next meeting would surely be interesting.

CHAPTER 26

Mike did not return to his office on Saturday or Sunday. He wasn't ready yet to confront Bonnie because he didn't know what to tell her. A part of him said the sleepover would not have any bearing on their working relationship, but somehow he found it difficult to believe this.

Bonnie stopped in on both Saturday and Sunday around noon, only to find an empty office. She understood his absence, but wished he had been there anyway.

On Monday morning, Bonnie came in at eight-thirty and found Mike talking with his associate, Don Burlingame, in the conference room. Mike noticed her arrival, but continued his discussion with Don. An hour later, he rose as Burlingame left the room and he called Bonnie over. She entered the conference room and noticed the piles of files on the long table.

"So, I guess you don't like omelets."

"Bonnie, it would have been wrong for me to stay. I think I'm moving too fast and I'm not really ready to get serious with anyone, not yet. Last Friday night was special to me, as I hope it was for you. But I think I need to focus on my work right now. Does this sound cruel? I don't mean it to be. But I just think we should slow down for a while, okay?"

"Mike, I'm not going anywhere if that is what you're worried about. I know that just because we slept together doesn't mean we're joined at the hip. If we are meant to be, it'll happen, whether it's now, next month, next year or whenever. But I want you to know you missed out on a great breakfast," she answered with a smile on her face. She wasn't going to be brushed aside without a fight.

December proved to be a very good month for Mike's firm as they settled five cases. There is a tendency at year-end for insurance settlements to be made. Insurance companies want claims removed from their potential liability list going forward. Budgeting for claims outstanding in the next calendar year is a cumbersome process, and insurance companies are willing to negotiate case settlements to get them off the books. He gave both Don Burlingame and Bonnie small bonuses before Christmas and hoped he would get a call from Mutual of New England before New Year's Day.

Playing a waiting game with law suit settlement offers wasn't enjoyable to Mike. He had hoped for some open dialogue with Kubaska after the November court decision, but Kubaska had not initiated any settlement talks.

On Tuesday, December 26th, Kubaska's associate, Ted Barrett, called Mike. He wanted to meet at his office in Providence to discuss a possible settlement of the class action suit. They agreed to meet the following day at two o'clock. When Barrett arrived, Mike greeted him with a handshake, and escorted him to the nearby conference room.

"Mr. Strange, first let me congratulate you on your excellent job in the first phase of the trial. You do realize, however, no one has ever won a negligence suit where radon was determined as the potential cause for lung cancer, no one! You also are aware, I'm sure, the time frame for a diagnosis of lung cancer from radon exposure is about twenty years, and this condo has only been in existence for about ten years. And many of the victims had not lived there for more than five years. So, I don't believe you have a strong enough case to convince a jury to find for the plaintiffs at trial in February, do you?"

"Well, Mr. Barrett, there's always a first time, isn't there? Twelve people died from lung cancer from the same condominium development in the last five years. Twelve, Mr. Barrett. None of them ever smoked a cigarette, were ever subjected to second-hand smoke in their work environment, nor had a family history of any cancer-causing death. And you want to sit there and tell me this is just a coincidence that exposure to extremely high levels of radon for years had nothing to do with it? Let's be serious here."

"Obviously, Mr. Strange, you have your opinions and my insurance company has its own. I came here today to see if we could settle this issue as two reasonable men, rather than burdening both our firms with a costly trial."

"I'm listening, Mr. Barrett."

"Mutual is willing to generously offer two million two hundred thousand dollars to settle the case. Three hundred thousand to each of the five plaintiffs who represent victims who lived in the condos for ten years, and one hundred thousand for each of the seven remaining plaintiffs who represent victims who lived there for less than seven years. This is a very generous offer, Mr. Strange, considering you may not get anything if you lose the case in February."

"You do realize we are asking for twelve million dollars in damages. You do also realize your own client, Jonathan Tate, offered to settle for nearly seven million before the trial even began."

"This is hearsay, Mr. Strange. Our client would deny any such offer, and you have nothing in writing to substantiate this claim."

"This is true, Mr. Barrett. All I have is the face to face word of a lying scumbag you call your client. He'd screw his own mother if he had to. Let's not try to bullshit our way through this. The man made me a verbal offer right here in this office and reneged on it the same day by not putting it in writing. Zero ethics, Mr. Barrett, that's what your client has…zero ethics."

"I'm not going to get into a debate on what is fact and what is fiction here. I've presented you with a good faith offer and need to know what I report back to Rupert Kubaska."

"I'll think about it and let you know. Naturally, I need to discuss this with my clients first. Give me a day or two to get back to you."

Barrett rose to leave and stretched out his hand to Mike. Reluctantly, Mike shook Barrett's hand and escorted him out the door.

Rather than subject each client to decide in front of the other plaintiffs, he decided to visit each one separately with

Barrett's offer. Almost all of them individually asked Mike, "What do you think, Mr. Strange? Is this a good settlement, or can we do better?" Ironically, eleven of the twelve had not even thought about a wrongful death claim against Tate Builders. They originally accepted their relative's death as natural. Were it not for the initial claim by Mrs. Collamati, there would be no law suit, nor the thought of any settlement. First, they had agreed to accept whatever the majority decided to do. Second, they were well-aware of Mike's costs to represent them. He would bear significant costs if the case went to trial and the plaintiffs lost. They almost all felt that the decision of whether to accept the offer or not should be left to Mike. Two of the clients were reluctant to risk losing several hundred thousand dollars, but they stayed true to their previous agreement....majority rules.

"Ted, Mike Strange. I'm afraid your offer to settle was rejected by my clients yesterday. They are willing to take their chances in court."

When Kubaska heard the news, he became adamant. "Who the hell does he think he's dealing with here? Damn it, let's get to work on preparing for trial, Ted. He didn't counter with his numbers, did he?" asked Kubaska.

"Not to me. But I'm sure he has a number. Want me to find out?"

"Wait until Friday. Then ask him for his best demand, one shot, period."

The radon case was still the largest one Mike had taken to trial, and the most costly. Expert witnesses, depositions, court fees, transcripts, and loads of other expenses mounted each day. If he lost the case at trial in February, he would end up deeply in debt. He had already taken out a second mortgage on his home in Cumberland, sold

Susan's car, and virtually exhausted any other savings they had accumulated. As New Year's Eve approached, it was no wonder he had not made plans to celebrate. This was his first New Year's Eve without Susan. His mind wandered to their attendance at a dinner dance at the Biltmore Hotel the year before. He and Susan had booked a room for the night so they wouldn't need to worry about a late night drive back to Cumberland if they had too much to drink. Gordie and Betty, their neighbors across the street, had booked a room next to Mike and Susan. Gordie's parents were babysitting their two small children overnight. Mike smiled as he recollected the night, but the smile disappeared as quickly as it came, and reality set in almost as fast as the disappearance of the memory.

At ten in the morning on the twenty-ninth of December, Mike received another call from Ted Barrett.

"Mike, have you thought about some counteroffer to the one I presented a few days ago? Rupert is willing to give you one shot at a final offer, the bottom line offer you're willing to accept. He doesn't want to go back and forth for the next month on this. So, it's either he thinks you're being reasonable, or we go to trial in February."

"Well, Ted, if he thinks I'm anywhere satisfied with somewhere close to the last offer of two million two hundred thousand, I won't waste my time or his."

"Give me a number, Mike. What's your bottom line?"

"Six million dollars. It's a half million for each plaintiff, half as much as we're asking for from the jurors, and less than Tate was willing to pay, even if he denies it. I know it, he knows it, and you can bet Rupert knows it too."

Mike closed his eyes, crossed his fingers, and bit his lip. He listened intently for any response from Barrett. The silence on the other end of the phone made Mike begin to sweat. His brow was perspiring as he reached for a tissue and wiped his forehead. Though the line was silent, he could hear some paper shuffling in the background. Then a voice suddenly returned in the receiver and simply said, "Mike, I'll get back to you on this. Are you in the office on Saturday?"

"Yes, I'll be in from nine to five Saturday." At that moment, all Mike could think of was *I blew it, I asked for too much.*

On Saturday, at one o'clock, Rupert Kubaska called.

"Good afternoon, Rupert. Are you getting ready for New Year's Eve tomorrow?" he asked as he picked up the phone.

"Hello, Mike. We have a few couples over to the house every year now for the last twenty years. I'm hoping we can put this to bed before my first cocktail. Look, I know Tate discussed a settlement with you in September. You and I know this should never have happened without counsel present. And, if I had been there, he never would have made such an offer. But he did, and I have to deal with him in my own way, even if he is a client. Mike, I simply can't go as high as six million. Can we come to some middle ground here? I'm willing to go to four million, but this is as high as I'll go, no more back and forth."

Mike was silent as he listened to Rupert's offer. He remained silent for about two full minutes as Rupert checked to make sure the connection was still open.

"Mike, are you there?"

"I'm here, Rupert. I'm thinking right now. Give me a minute or two here."

Mike got up from his desk and began to silently cheer with his fist pumping in the air. Everyone in the office could see him pumping his fist wildly like a pro golfer who just sank a thirty-foot putt to win a tournament. He then returned to his desk, sat down, and picked up the receiver.

"Rupert, you know, I've got a really solid case here and twelve people are dead from Rock Ridge Common. What value you place on a life lost before its time is hard to say. But going through another long trial isn't going to bring those people back, and their survivors have suffered enough. I'll accept your offer of four million, subject to my clients' formal agreement, which I do not believe will be a problem."

Mike wished Kubaska a good year in 1990 and hung up the phone. He paraded into the main office and announced to Bonnie and Don that the radon case had just been settled. In his right hand was a bottle of champagne, and in his left were three wine glasses. Bonnie was especially pleased to hear the news. She had the scars to prove how stressful the case had been, and she knew what a relief this was to Mike.

At two o'clock, he called each of the plaintiffs to inform them of the settlement. Each one would receive $233,333 after deducting Mike's thirty percent contingency fee of $100,000 per plaintiff. The $1.2 million fee was the largest he would receive since he began his practice. His clients were ecstatic at the news.

After he had spoken to all the clients, he wished his staff a Happy New Year and prepared to leave the office, not expecting to return until the following Tuesday, January 2. As he put on his topcoat, he whispered to Bonnie.

"Can I call you this weekend?"

"Well, I don't know," she stated with a smile. "I'll check my social calendar. It's New Year's Eve tomorrow, you know."

"So, are you overbooked?"

"I guess I can squeeze you in somewhere. Give me a call."

* * *

Judge Cromwell gave his blessing to the settlement on Monday morning, February nineteenth. The jurors had been summoned in the morning by the judge's clerk, and waited upstairs in the jury room, expecting to begin the medical phase of the trial.

In his chambers, Judge Cromwell said to Mike, "You did a good thing for these people, Mr. Strange. They could have ended up with nothing at all when you consider there's never been a suit won in a radon case yet," said Cromwell. "Because of the settlement, there's still no case to have been won where radon was involved. Someday though, I think the streak will end."

CHAPTER 27

On Friday, September 2, 2011, American Airlines Flight 1654 from San Francisco landed at Green Airport in Warwick, Rhode Island. Mike Strange and his partner, Bonnie Stevens, had made this flight often in the last ten years, every time they returned to Providence from their home on the island of Maui, in Hawaii. Although he was still the controlling partner in his firm, Mike had long since relinquished the day-to-day management to Don Burlingame. The personal injury market for attorneys had grown substantially since Mike first started practicing in the late 1980s. His agreement with Burlingame was to meet on or about the first business day after Labor Day each year for a full day of reviewing active cases in the firm's three offices. On occasion, the review took part of a second day as well when the caseload was greater. But the rest of the year, Mike would communicate with the firm extensively through email messages and occasional telephone conferences from his home in the Hana area of the island.

Bonnie and Mike had never married, but continued to live together since the early-1990s, some twenty years earlier. They made a point to meet Susan's parents for dinner at least on one occasion when they were in town. Mike still owned a condominium in Berkshire Estates, and he and Bonnie stayed there during this week each year. The rest of the time, the condo was available for clients of the firm, as needed.

Samantha and Alex remembered the conversation with Susan's parents about Mike's visit to Providence around Labor Day. She kept looking at the calendar as each day in August passed and the Labor Day weekend approached. On Thursday, September 1, Samantha got on her cell phone and called Alice Pennington.

"Mrs. Pennington, this is Samantha Collins. Do you remember me? I interviewed you and your husband with my friend Alex Brien about an article I was doing about your daughter Susan for the Northeastern newspaper, *The Huntington News*?" she began.

"Yes, of course, how are you?"

"Mrs. Pennington, you had mentioned to us that Mike Strange would be in the area sometime around Labor Day. Is that still happening? I'd love to interview him too if he can squeeze us in?"

"Well, we'll be dining with him on Saturday. I'll mention it to him and see what he says. Give me a number where I can reach you on Sunday and I'll let you know," Alice answered.

When Ralph and Alice met Mike and Bonnie at Hemenway's Restaurant in Providence on Saturday, Alice mentioned Samantha's request to Mike.

"Why is she doing an article about Susan? It's been over twenty years," he asked.

"Because Susan was a former graduate of Northeastern, and she thought students would find the article interesting since the case remains unsolved. When we met her about a month ago, she was very nice. She and her boyfriend had spent some time with Ed Lemoine in Cumberland going over the files. Who knows, maybe a set of fresh eyes on the files might help. I've sort of considered it a lost cause by now anyway."

"What do you think, Bonnie?" he asked.

"If it's the same guy who rammed my car and nearly killed me back then, maybe she'll find more than Ed has been able to after all these years," she answered. "And besides, you know as well as I, Mike, you'll never rest until this is resolved once and for all. It won't hurt to talk to her while we're here. We don't leave until Friday."

"Okay. Mom, let her know I'll meet with her at the condo on Tuesday afternoon around three o'clock. I should be done at the firm by then."

Samantha welcomed the news of the scheduled meeting with enthusiasm. She called Alex and he agreed to drive them to the condo on Bear Hill Road in Cumberland that afternoon. As they approached the unit, Samantha suddenly became very nervous. She was about to confront someone she believed was her husband in a former life. Alex tried to calm her, but he could sense the anxiety in her face as they rang the doorbell.

Bonnie opened the door and greeted them. Mike was mixing himself a drink on the kitchen counter and walked heartily over to greet them.

"Samantha, Alex, can I get you a drink? I was just making myself one. A glass of wine, soda, something stronger? I'm a martini guy myself. Bonnie is a wine drinker."

"I'm a wine drinker too," said Alex. "Samantha likes vodka gimlets, but wine is fine for both of us, thanks."

"You are the first woman I've met since my late wife who likes vodka gimlets," Mike replied. "Where in the world did you acquire a taste for that drink?" he asked as he stared at Samantha.

"I really don't know. I think it was at a bar in the South End of Boston at the end of last year after a show at the Wang Center," she replied.

"Wow, does that take me back a few years. Susan and I had done the same thing back in the eighties. Our favorite spot was O'Toole's Irish Tavern on Tremont Street," Mike answered.

"You're kidding. It's still there, Mr. Strange, still going strong and still run by Sean O'Toole and his wife. She's the one who introduced me to the gimlet," added Samantha.

"What a coincidence," Bonnie chimed in. "Shall we have a seat in the living room?"

As they sat down, Mike brought in two glasses of white wine and placed them on the end table next to their chairs. He returned moments later with his martini and another wine for Bonnie.

"So, folks, what's this article about Susan? It's been quite a while since 1989."

Samantha had difficulty when she tried to look directly at Mike when she spoke. She felt his look penetrate her entire body every time he looked her way. It was as if she could guess his every move.

"Mr. Strange," Alex began. "Do you still believe, after all these years, the case will ever be solved and the killer will ever be brought to justice?"

"Doesn't look like it, does it? Every year I call Ed Lemoine for an update, and every year I hear the same news, nothing. I've always thought the Tates had something to do with her death, but the police weren't able to connect them at all."

"If you suddenly had a lead on the case after all these years, would that bring you back to the Mainland to see it through? I realize breaking away from you're A-frame on the beach in Hana wouldn't be easy?" Samantha asked.

"If there was something new on the case, I'd be here... we'd be here in a heartbeat, Samantha. How did you know we lived in an A-frame in Hana anyway?"

"Oh, your mother-in-law must have mentioned it to us last month when we were at her house," Samantha blurted, surprised by Mike's curiosity about her comment.

"Ah, she would know. They stayed with us last summer for about a month. She realized then why Susan and I had always said we'd have a home in Hana someday," Mike answered.

"But even if a new lead was found in the case, I don't know where it would go. All the active people from 1989 were checked out pretty thoroughly back then."

"Suppose there was an eye witness who suddenly said he or she saw the killer commit the crime but was too afraid to come forward. And now, for whatever reason, this person can't live with this information any more. What would you say to this, Mr. Strange?" asked Samantha.

"I'd say it would be my lucky day, Samantha. But I live in the real world where I deal with facts and proof in all my cases. I don't believe in luck and, after twenty years, the odds of something new popping up all of a sudden are quite slim."

Samantha and Alex told Mike they would mail him a copy of the article after it was published. Mike in turn gave them a post office box in Hana where the article could be sent. After they left the condo, Mike looked at Bonnie and said.

"She knows something about the case she's not telling us, Bonnie. I can feel it. Something about our interest if new evidence was found. Maybe I'm imagining things, but I think I'll go see Ed Lemoine tomorrow. I want to check the case file one more time. Want to come?"

"Sure, I've never really looked at the file myself in all these years."

Samantha sat in Alex's car, fastened her seat belt, and asked him to stop for coffee at Phantom Farms. She remembered the location of the store as they pulled into the gravel parking lot.

"Alex, it was him, I'm certain now. I was married to Mike Strange years ago. This is how I knew so much about Northeastern when I first visited the school. It was Susan's memory I was reliving. If I tell him this, he'll think I'm crazy. I'd probably feel the same way. How do I tell somebody I was his wife who was murdered years ago and I can identify who did it if I see his picture?"

"Sammy. We've got to go back to the police station. Let's see if there are people mentioned in the case file who didn't arouse anybody's attention back then. Maybe see if we can find photos of all those people. The station is right down the road. If Lemoine isn't there, we can come back another day."

Following the short drive to the station, Ed Lemoine was still on duty and would have brought the file back upstairs had he known they were coming. After he retrieved the file box, he asked.

"Is there anything in particular you want to look at again?"

"Anything to do with the Tates' alibi, who attested to their whereabouts, pictures of anyone associated with them, stuff like that would be helpful," Samantha answered.

"Well, Larry Resta, a foreman for Tate, said they both were at Rusty Pines in Uxbridge. Carl Hannigan and Manny Dominguez, two other workers at the work site, said they talked to both Tate brothers at the time also."

"What about other Tate relatives? Brothers, cousins, anybody like that?" Alex asked.

"Let's see here. Well, the Tates had a sister who was married to the owner of the engineering company they used once in a while. And Jonathan Tate's wife has a brother, Zeke Goodman, who worked for the Tates, but he wasn't around here the week of the murder. As a matter of fact, I don't think he's around here now. I think he's in Florida somewhere."

"Any photos of these guys?" Samantha asked.

"Not that I'm aware of. Why the sudden interest in photos of all these guys?"

"We just would like to know who we're talking about, that's all."

"I can get you a mug shot of Goodman. He has a prison record and was released about three months before the murder."

"But no one tried to contact him for questioning?" Samantha asked. "I'd like a copy of his file and any address for this guy, if you have one. I'd also like addresses for the other three guys too. I don't suppose you have pictures of them, do you?"

Ed Lemoine felt somewhat embarrassed at the implication of possible oversights in his investigation years earlier. What should have been obvious follow-up procedures in the investigation were brought to his attention by two inexperienced observers. The mug shot of Zeke Goodman was only a photo of his face. In the photo, Zeke's hair was shoulder length, and he had a full beard. As Samantha read his criminal file, she noticed a section on distinguishing marks, identifying a small scar on his chin from an altercation in a bar in 1983, shortly before his five-year conviction in the state penitentiary for armed robbery.

"Is this the only photo you have of Goodman?" she asked.

"Yes, but I can email you others after I get a copy of his whole file, if you want?" Lemoine answered.

"Yes, please."

When they left the station, Samantha appeared to be in a daze.

"Sammy, are you okay?" Alex asked.

"Goodman has a scar on his chin, Alex. I wonder if he has tattoos too. I can't really get a clear look at his face on the picture because of his beard."

"Are you sure?"

"No, I'm not, not from this picture, but maybe if he sends me more pictures, I'll know then."

CHAPTER 28

Mike was anxious to see Ed Lemoine at the Cumberland police station on Wednesday morning. He and Bonnie arrived at nine o'clock and Lemoine was surprised by the visit.

"Mike, what in the world are you doing here? I thought you were still in Hawaii."

"No, this is my annual visit to meet with my partner who handles the day-to-day operations of the firm. We head back on Friday," Mike answered. "This is Bonnie Stevens, Ed. You may remember I told you about Bonnie."

"Very nice to meet you at last, Bonnie. Mike has talked about you for the last ten years, but I thought you were a figment of his imagination. So, folks, I wish I had something to report to you, but I don't."

"Ed, what can you tell me about these two young people from Northeastern looking into Susan's case? I met them yesterday, and I got the feeling they might be on to something."

"What did you tell them yesterday? They were here at the station looking through the files again around three thirty. The Samantha girl asked some pretty interesting questions. She focused on anyone associated with the Tates," Lemoine said.

"She deliberately asked me if I would return to the Mainland if there was a break in the case. This is a strange question for someone to ask, especially someone I've never met before. What exactly did she focus on, Ed?" asked Mike.

"You know, Mike, she kind of gave me hell for not pursuing Jonathan Tate's brother-in-law, Zeke Goodman. After I showed her his mug shot, she wanted to know if there were other photos of him elsewhere."

"Mug shot, are you telling me this Goodman guy has a record, Ed?" Mike asked with a puzzled look on his face.

"Yeah, he had been in the state pen for about five years for armed robbery in 1979 and finished his parole quite a while ago. We couldn't connect with him at all during the months after the murder, and all the information we got from Tate was that he lived in Orlando. We've never seen him, nor have we any reason to believe he was around here at the time."

"You mean to tell me there was a brother-in-law with a record for armed robbery and you just took Tate's word he wasn't here when Susan was killed? Are you kidding me? Why wasn't I ever told about this Zeke Goodman before? Jesus, Ed, and this is who Samantha Collins focused on?" Mike moaned in utter disappointment.

"Let me see everything you showed her. And give me copies of everything you gave her. She knows something, Ed. She's just doing an article for the school newspaper on the unsolved case? Bullshit, there's more to this. I can sense it."

Once Lemoine had given the information Mike requested, he insisted he be informed of any further contact with Samantha. Bonnie had scanned Zeke Goodman's rap sheet and found nothing more than had been discussed so far, until her eyes zeroed in on a line in his file entitled "Vehicle". Next to the title was "1987 Chevy blue pickup truck." Bonnie's eyes were fixated on this line when Mike could see the look on her face.

"Bonnie, what's wrong? What are you pointing at?" Mike asked.

"His vehicle, Mike. The guy drove a blue pickup truck," she yelled.

"So what?"

"So, like a blue pickup truck that rammed me off the road that summer, that's what."

"Ed, did you guys follow-up on this guy at all?"

"No, not really. Mike, the incident in North Smithfield was under their jurisdiction, and we don't know anything about her car crash in 1989," Lemoine shrugged.

"Ed, I need a favor. This might be a long-shot, but can you get a list of all the body shops in 1989 within a ten to fifteen mile radius of North Smithfield? If one of these guys has any record of a truck repair for Zeke Goodman, we may be lucky."

"Wow, this is a tall order, Mike. I'll need to get my captain to okay this. I'm not too optimistic he'll agree to spend the manpower for all this work after so long. And it still doesn't necessarily connect the car incident with Susan's murder."

As Mike and Bonnie left the station, they looked at each other and Bonnie said, "I don't think we'll be on a plane to Hawaii on Friday, will we?"

"I'll call Don at the office and tell him we'll be staying at the condo a little while longer, so he doesn't commit it to someone else for now," Mike answered.

"Bonnie, we can't just wait for Ed to get the go-ahead on this. Ask him for the name of a body shop guy who's been in the business around here for over twenty years, and we'll start there. These guys tend to know each other, and refer jobs to each other when they've got too much to handle."

She began her investigation on Thursday morning, and was able to get a list of ten body shops that were in business in 1989. One by one, she visited these shops asking about Zeke Goodman and a blue pickup truck. Most shops did not keep records this far back, nor did they recognize Zeke Goodman's name...not until she came to number nine on her list, Frank's Body Shop and Auto Sales in Bellingham, Massachusetts.

"Zeke Goodman, are you kidding me? Is this a name from the past or what," Frank Mohan, the owner, chanted.

"I bet I haven't heard that name in twenty years. It's good to know he's still alive. He is still alive, isn't he?"

At first, Bonnie didn't know what to say. She didn't know him, but obviously Frank Mohan did.

"I never met the man, quite honestly," she replied. "I'm just following up on an incident which occurred in 1989 where he might have had some body work done on a pickup truck."

"Sure did. He bought the truck from me right around that time, and he needed cash to get to Florida. So, I bought it back from him in September of the same year after fixing it up before I resold it to my nephew."

"What was wrong with it? You said you had to fix it first."

"Front bumper was all bent and he wanted to paint it a different color, black I think. No sooner than I finish the job for him, he asks me if I'm interested in buying it back because he was leaving for Orlando, I think, and was driving down with another guy. They were going to work for a builder down there. I remember he told me he was going to buy another truck when he got there, but needed a few pay checks under his belt first."

"You wouldn't have a record of those repairs somewhere would you? I know it's been a long time."

"Hell, yes, ma'am, I have kept records of every vehicle I've worked on since 1975, over thirty-five years now. You can come back tomorrow and I'll have a copy for you. The 1989 records are up there in the attic. It'll take me a while to find the box," Mohan answered.

"Who'd you say you worked for?"

"I'm with Michael Strange and Associates in Providence. The vehicle may have been involved in an accident back then. Thanks for your help, I'll be back tomorrow," Bonnie said with excitement in her voice.

She took out her cell phone and called Mike as she left the body shop.

"Mike, I found the place in Bellingham. Get this, he's still got the repair records and said I could pick up a copy tomorrow. What are you up to?"

"I'm trying to get hold of either Goodman's 1989 tax filing or his employment records at Tate Builders. If he

worked there in 1988 or 1989, he'd be listed on the Form
901s which Tate would have filed each quarter back then.
I've got a friend at the IRS in Providence. I handled a personal injury case a few years ago for his wife. She got pretty
banged up when a drunk driver rammed her car broadside
one night on her way home from work. They got a pretty
good settlement out of it," he said.

"I still can't believe Ed never followed up on this guy
back then. Anyway, I told my friend why I needed this
information. He didn't promise anything, but the IRS in
Providence keep stuff almost forever. We'll see. I cancelled
the flight back for now. I hate for you to relive the terrible
incident that almost killed you, Bonnie, but what if Susan's
murder and your hit-and-run are related?" he said.

"What puzzles me, Mike, is how this girl knew enough
to zero in on Goodman to begin with. This is more than
just an article for a college newspaper, I'll bet on it. I simply
can't put my finger on it," Bonnie replied.

"Bonnie, I'm thinking of trying to meet with
Samantha Collins tomorrow in Boston. Ed gave me her
address and I got her phone number from Alice earlier
today. Maybe without her boyfriend there and you as
well, maybe she'll tell me more about what she knows.
At this stage, I've got nothing to lose by confronting her.
What do you think?"

"I'm on my way back to the condo now. Why don't we
talk about it then?"

On Friday morning, right after they had breakfast
around eight o'clock, Mike kissed Bonnie goodbye as
he prepared to drive to Northeastern University to meet
Samantha. They had decided not to call her ahead of time
to avoid Samantha from having Alex there by her side. Mike

was certain there was something curious about Samantha. She had been the one asking more aggressive questions and the one grilling Ed Lemoine for information on Zeke Goodman.

"Call me if you come up with anything," Bonnie said. "I'll pick up that information on Goodman's truck repair this afternoon."

CHAPTER 29

The knock on her dormitory apartment door startled Samantha. Who could be calling at eleven in the morning? As she opened the door, her face flushed with a surprised look as Mike Strange stood facing her.

"Hello, Samantha. I'm sorry I didn't call ahead of time, but I wanted a chance to talk to you again after our meeting on Tuesday afternoon."

"Oh, uh, actually Mr. Strange, we have plenty of material for the *Huntington News* article. So, it really isn't necessary for us to get more," Samantha blurted hesitantly.

"I'm not here about that, Samantha. I'm here about your interest in Zeke Goodman. I was with Ed Lemoine on Wednesday, and he told me all about your interest in Tate's brother-in-law. Can I come in, please? If you feel uncomfortable with me coming in, perhaps we can go to a coffee shop if it will put you more at ease?" he asked.

Samantha still had difficulty making eye contact with Mike. He made her nervous, and she realized he was aware of this. The suggestion to talk in a more public setting was enticing, but Samantha invited Mike in anyway. She wasn't afraid of him. After all, this was her husband in a former life, not that Mike had any inkling of this.

"Can I get you a cup of coffee, a soda, or something?"

"No, I'm fine, but feel free to have something yourself if you want. I might have one later," Mike answered.

"Samantha, be honest with me. Your interest in Susan doesn't really have anything to do with just an article on some Northeastern grad from twenty something years ago, does it?"

"What do you mean, Mr. Strange? Of course it does. Why else would I put such an article together?"

"I met with Christine Ettoya earlier this morning at her office, and asked her about the article. She told me the idea came from you. She knew nothing about Susan's murder, and said you've never submitted anything for the college newspaper before. How do you know anything about Susan? What prompted you to recommend the article to begin with? Please, this was my wife we're talking about here."

Samantha's face again became flushed, but this time she couldn't come up with a response quick enough. Mike sensed her uneasiness.

"If you know anything about her murder, Samantha, please let me in on this. Your questions to me and to Ed Lemoine about her murder are far more than some information to put an article together. They're more investigating than just gathering information. Please, Samantha."

She rose from her chair in the kitchen and stared out her dorm window at the Boston skyline.

"First of all, Mr. Strange, what I'm about to tell you will sound bizarre and you'll probably think I'm nuts. But I can assure you, the last time I checked, I was perfectly sane, odd maybe, but sane," Samantha began.

"Do you believe in reincarnation, Mr. Strange, the ability for someone to have lived as someone else in a previous life?"

"I can't say that I know much about the theory, at least I'm not aware of any known cases on the subject. I do remember seeing a movie in the 70s called *The Reincarnation of Peter Proud* with Michael Sarazen, but that's about it," he answered.

"I was born in June, 1989 in Hoboken, New Jersey. My parents were both from the area too. When I was thirteen, I started having nightmares about a woman's murder. I didn't know who the woman was, where she lived, or when she was murdered. My parents were concerned and took me to see a sleep psychologist. He determined I must have seen the murder on a TV show or read about it somewhere, and it stuck in my mind. He said the dream would likely go away over time. But it didn't. Over the next few years, it got worse." Samantha started to feel more at ease as she turned to face Mike.

"At eighteen, when my parents took me to see some colleges in Boston, I knew the Northeastern campus like I had lived here before. I knew where everything was, even though I had never been here. Do you know how weird that feels?"

Mike was silent as he listened intently to Samantha's story. He focused now on her every move and word.

"This spring, my boyfriend Alex and I went to a concert at PPAC in Providence. On the way down Route 95, we ran into a tie-up in Attleboro. There was a sign telling people to take Route 295 to Route 146 to avoid delays getting into Providence. Once we were on Route 295, I recognized a sign for Phantom Farms in Cumberland, even though I had never been to Rhode Island. We took the exit and the place looked familiar to me, but I couldn't remember why. When we headed back to Route 295, I saw a sign for Burke Road, and again I recognized the name. When we passed your former house, Mr. Strange, I knew the house. I knew the layout inside, the St. Joseph statue buried under the dining room window, how the master bedroom looked, everything."

Mike rose from his chair and couldn't believe what he was hearing. Before he spoke, Samantha continued.

"You see, Mr. Strange, I'm finding out I was Susan in a life before mine. Sounds crazy, I know, but I can prove it. My parents were Ralph and Alice Pennington, and when we visited their home last month, I knew this is where I was brought up. My bedroom was the same as when I lived there and Alice was as much my mother then as she was over forty years ago."

"Whoa, whoa here. What the hell are you saying?"

"I'm saying everything I remember now is about Susan Pennington Strange, the girl you met on a commuter train in Attleboro. The girl you proposed to in your last year of law school. The girl you eloped with to Hawaii in 1988 where you both fell in love with Hana in Maui. And the girl who remembers what her murderer looks like. That's what I'm saying, Mr. Strange."

Mike fell back in his chair and look stunned. He was speechless for ever so long. Then he became suspicious of Samantha's claims and started asking questions.

"How do I know you haven't just done some thorough research on our lives?" he blurted.

"For what purpose? Why and how could I fabricate all these details of who I was if it didn't really happen? How do I know you love your martinis with three olives, no less, no more? How do I know you hate tying a necktie and never wear a buttoned-down shirt?"

"Stop it, stop. This is incredible. You are asking me to believe you were my wife Susan in a previous life. That's crazy. I've never heard of anything like this. There has to be some other explanation, ESP, a medium, somebody who's been given a gift like this."

"You don't get it, Mr. Strange. She's the only one I know about, no one else, and I seem to remember more each day. I have no explanation for knowing all of this. I can assure you, I'm not nuts and I have no motive here. This has tormented me for too long. It has to come out. If I see this man in my dreams, this guy with a scar on his chin and a tattoo of a horse's face on his arm, I will know him. Do you understand? Do I think this might be Zeke Goodman? I don't know. I never met the man. The pictures of him so far are with a beard and show only his face, nothing else. Could he be the one? Maybe. Now you know why I'm curious who this man is, where he is, and how I get to rule him out of the picture. Until then, this is driving me crazy, and believe me, Mr. Strange, I'm not crazy."

Samantha walked over to her desk in the corner of the room, grabbed a stack of papers, and handed them to Mike.

"You tell me, after you read these articles, if this can't happen. These people all knew about their lives in another time and as someone else, especially the Indian woman," she said.

As Mike reached for the articles, his cell phone rang.

"Hey, Mike, how did you make out with Samantha Collins?" Bonnie asked.

"It's complicated, Bonnie, very complicated. I can't talk about this on the phone. I'll see you later this afternoon."

"Well, okay, but aren't you interested in knowing how I made out?"

"Oh, sure. Did you get the repair bill?"

"You bet, and guess what? Goodman had the truck painted black. But the repair guy told me the blue paint underneath wasn't removed. They just painted over it. And get this; his nephew still has the truck. His family uses it at their home on Lake Winnipesaukee in New Hampshire to plow the snow from their long driveway when they go up there skiing. If we get a paint chip sample from the truck, it might match the sample the police removed from my rear bumper in '89," Bonnie explained excitedly.

"I've got a lot more, Bonnie, an awful lot more. I'm still here, but I should be on the road soon. We've got a lot to talk about. Oh, by the way, see if the body shop remembers what this Goodman looked like."

Once he hung up the line and put his cell phone back in his sport coat, he sighed. He sat down on the sofa and stared down at the floor in silence.

"What is my favorite color?"

"Blue."

"Do you know of any injuries I had when we were at Northeastern together?"

"Do you mean the pins they put in your left ankle after the skiing accident on Mt. Snow?"

The silence that followed lasted for nearly ten minutes. Samantha knew how all of this sounded. She could feel his pain at the re-enactment of events only Susan would know about. The more she revealed, the clearer her memory was. She began to feel the burden of these memories lifted from her conscience, a feeling not felt since the dreams began as an early teenager. She sat next to him and reached for his hand.

"I wish this had never happened to me, Mr. Strange, but it did. And if what I know can bring peace and justice to you somehow, it will have been worth it."

A few minutes later, Mike rose from the sofa and turned to Samantha.

"Would you be available for dinner with Bonnie and me tonight at our place?" Mike almost pleaded. "I don't think I can explain all of this to her without you being there."

"Can I bring Alex with me? He knows as much as you do about this. I didn't tell you we visited your office the day I saw the house. The lady who lives there told us your name and how you had an office in Providence. We were going to PPAC anyway, and when I passed the building your office was in, I knew it was you from the pictures in your brochure. Do I look like her?"

"Yes and no. Yes, Alex is certainly invited too. And no, you don't look at all like Susan. That would have really freaked me out."

CHAPTER 30

"Do you think he believes you were his wife years ago?" Alex asked Samantha as they rode toward Cumberland. Commuter traffic on Route 95 South at five o'clock was very slow. It seemed like Alex came to a full stop almost every five minutes or so.

"He realized I knew things about him no one else could. He doesn't want to believe me, but I've made it difficult for him to argue. This is so weird, Alex. Put yourself in his position and how you would react to a perfect stranger telling you things only your dead wife would know. Then tell him you are his dead wife reincarnated into a new body. Er, you will tell them I'm not crazy, won't you?" Samantha asked with some doubt on her lingering comment about her sanity.

"A bit odd at times, maybe, but surely playing with a full deck, Sammy," Alex joked.

She could feel her stomach in knots as they approached the condominium. *I've got to get this over with,* she thought. *I can't tell you how relieved I am this is finally coming out.*

Bonnie greeted them at the door as they entered. Mike was standing with his back to them as he gazed at the fire from the gas fireplace. There was an unusual chill in the air for early September. Perhaps it was more from being away from the tropical climate of Hawaii, or perhaps it was Mike's anxiety at this meeting that brought about the chill. As he turned to welcome them, he spoke.

"I feel as though, under the circumstances, Samantha, you should probably start calling me Mike instead of Mr. Strange, if that's okay with you?"

"Mike it is then. But let me clear up a few things if I may? My recollection of your wife's life is just that to me, a recollection. I don't have any emotional feelings for you as I'm sure your wife had for you when she was alive. I just remember things about her life no one else does, except maybe you, Mike. Alex here is my only love interest in this life, more so now than ever before," Samantha answered as she held Alex's hand very tightly.

"Mr. Strange, it's been very hard for me to understand all of this," Alex began. "But I've been with her through every new discovery on this, and I can assure you, this is not some crazy woman just ranting about having been someone else before she was born in New Jersey in 1989. And there are medical records from her doctor years ago of her teen-age nightmares. The rest of the story blew my mind as she told me where to turn to get to your house, how she ran up to the front door, how she knew your face from the law firm brochure, and the tears that flowed from her cheeks when we left the Pennington's. You just don't make this stuff up."

"Neither of you have to convince me further. Bonnie did that for me when I got home this afternoon. When she called me when I was still at your place this afternoon in Boston, Samantha, the last thing I said to her was to ask the body shop guy if he remembered what Goodman looked like," Mike stated.

"Bonnie, you tell them what he said."

"Well, he was surprised I called him back since I had just left his place a half hour before. But when I asked him the question, he told me Zeke Goodman looked like a tough guy, like a prize fighter who'd been in one too many fights. He had a scar on his chin which looked like it had been there for a while. When I told Mike about it, he didn't think it was a big deal, until I told him about the tattoo. Mohan remembers Goodman told him how much he liked horses when he was a kid. He liked horses so much so, he had the face of a horse tattooed on his left arm below the elbow. There is no way you could have known this, Samantha, no way," Bonnie stared at Samantha.

"Finally," Samantha sighed. "We've got to find him. I'll know him when I see him. I've seen his face for nearly eight years now, and if it is Goodman, he has to be caught somehow. No one will ever believe me or my story, and I'm not about to become a sideshow for the media on this. No one outside this room can ever know. Is that clear?"

"He did work for Tate Builders in 1989. My friend at the IRS said his name was included in the company's quarterly wage report for the first and second quarter of that year. He wasn't listed anywhere after that, or on any Tate tax reports," Mike said.

"So, he was around when Susan was murdered?" Samantha said.

"He still lives in the Orlando area according to his 2010 tax return. He works as a foreman for Pelican Homes. And I've got his last address," Mike added.

Bonnie held up her hand. As she flashed four airline tickets on Southwest for Friday afternoon, she said. "The only way we know for sure is to go to Orlando and see if Zeke Goodman is still around. In the meantime, I've contacted the North Smithfield police, and they'll get a blue paint sample from the truck in New Hampshire. If it matches Goodman's truck, we're one step closer. I can't believe this is happening after all this time."

* * *

Samantha and Alex didn't hesitate to accept the tickets. There was no way she would miss an opportunity to get this guy out of her dreams, and a direct confrontation might just do the trick, she thought. Following dinner with Mike and Bonnie, they left for Boston to pack enough clothes as if they were going on a week's vacation. Their senior year at Northeastern would begin in a few weeks, and both of them were aware of the amount of time they had available before their first classes. What better way to spend a week in Florida than to hunt for a murderer.

They met Mike and Bonnie at Green Airport in Warwick at eleven o'clock on Friday morning. Bonnie had rented an executive home in Windermere Estates in Orlando. The unit had three bedrooms, a heated pool, and all the amenities they needed for their stay in the Florida area. The one o'clock flight would arrive in Orlando at three-thirty. The rental SUV would take them to the rented house a half hour from the airport.

When they arrived at their destination, the first thing Bonnie did was search for a local phonebook. She spotted one on the kitchen counter next to a wall phone and started thumbing through it.

"Goodman, Goodman, Goodman," she murmured as her fingers scanned the names on the page.

"Ah, Goodman, Ezekiel, 343 Lakeview Terrace, Kissimmee. Guess where we'll be around six tomorrow morning? If he's still in construction work for Pelican Homes, chances are they work on Saturdays, and it's likely they start around seven and finish around three in the afternoon," Bonnie added.

"We should take a ride to Lakeview Terrace while it's still light out, so we know how to get there tomorrow. I brought my GPS with me, and I'll set it up now," Mike answered.

"Suppose it is the same guy in my dreams, Mike. What do we do next?" Samantha asked. "I'm not exactly sure how we get to prove he did this twenty years ago."

"We take one step at a time, Samantha. I've waited this long for something to happen. I can wait a little longer. We'll figure it out as we go along.

CHAPTER 31

Larry Pelican, the owner of Pelican Homes in Orlando, had served with Jonathan Tate in the military in the early eighties. So, when Zeke Goodman applied for a job as a heavy equipment operator at Pelican Homes, it was no surprise that Zeke had listed Jonathan as a reference on his application form.

Zeke got the job and began working in late August, 1989. Pelican had called Tate to get more information on Zeke. Jonathan told him Goodman was his brother-in-law, had been a heavy-equipment operator for him for several months, but wanted to live in a warmer climate. The move to Florida had been a planned one according to Jonathan.

When Pelican hired Zeke, he noticed how muscular he was and how his rugged mannerism would fit perfectly working as a bouncer at his nightclub, The Kitty Lounge. Pelican arranged for Zeke to rent one of the apartments at one of the complexes he owned, and Zeke quickly settled into the Orlando area.

Zeke would work at Pelican Homes' worksites by day until three, and from eight until one in the morning on Friday and Saturday nights at the club. This is where he bumped into an old ex-con buddy one night at the bar. Danny Scott had been released from prison following a five-year sentence for grand theft-auto. Old habits never die, and Danny couldn't wait to get back into the business of stealing cars for a living. He needed someone to handle fencing the cars and asked Zeke to join him.

So, Zeke had his hands in many different ventures from 1989 to 2011. He started to rake in quite a bit of income, most of it undetected and unreported. He had bought a house in a gated community in Kissimmee, and had married Pelican's only daughter, Marsha, in 2005.

As should have been expected, Zeke was not a good husband. He fooled around with more than one of the dancers from the club. Marsha knew this from the scent of perfume on his clothes, or the occasional lipstick stains on his shirt collars when she did the laundry. She had grown to fear Zeke, and although he had never physically harmed her, she lived with the fear that he would turn nasty one day. Yet, she never said anything to her father. Instead, she preoccupied herself with golf and tennis. The tennis pro at the Laguna Tennis Club, adjacent to the Orlando Hills Country Club, had given Marsha more than just tennis lessons. Their after-tennis interludes in the ladies' locker room were obvious to most other women members. Marsha was ten years younger than Zeke, and their separate lives appeared to be a convenient arrangement. Fortunately, they had no children to interfere with their loose lifestyles.

"Sergeant Ed Lemoine, please. Tell him it's Mike Strange calling."

"Hi, Mike, any more news?"

"Ed, we're in Orlando, tracking down the last address we have on Zeke Goodman. I need a favor," Mike asked.

"Anything I can do to help."

"The guy lives in a gated community and we can't get into the complex because of the security guards at the entrance. Through the police network, is there a way for you to see if he has cars registered at his address?"

"Let me get this straight. You're looking for any cars registered to Goodman at his local address in Florida? What's that going to do?"

"If we see a car with a certain license plate entering the complex, we'll know enough to follow it from a distance and see who's driving it when the car leaves. I guess it's what you guys would call a stakeout. The sooner we get a make, model, and license plate, the sooner we're in business."

"Be careful, Mike. If this guy is the same one who murdered Susan, and he finds out you're following him, no telling what he's capable of doing next."

"The faster we flush this guy out, the sooner we can go to the local police for help."

"I'll see what I can find out. I've got your cell number. Keep it on all the time," Lemoine replied.

Late Friday afternoon, all four left in the rented SUV after Mike had punched in Goodman's address in the GPS system. Surprisingly, the location was only a few miles away. They then decided to go to a nearby restaurant for an early dinner. Friday nights in the Orlando area meant long lines at most restaurants if you got there at six o'clock or later. At five o'clock, following their flight from Warwick, the drive to the rental house, and the tension of beginning the search for Goodman, dinner sounded like a good plan. This would enable them to get back to their unit early in the evening and talk about their strategy if Goodman was indeed the man in Samantha's dreams for the last seven years. They had no clue what they would do next to bring this guy to justice. Just knowing who he was, this clearly would not be enough to satisfy Mike.

No sooner than they returned to their rented house, Mike's cellphone rang. He leaped for the phone on the kitchen counter.

"Mike, this is Ed. Grab a pencil and paper," Lemoine said. "There are two vehicles registered at that address. One is to Ezekiel Goodman, a 2001 black Mercedes C-250, and license number 648-312. The other is to a Marsha Goodman, a 2008 red Mazda Miata, and license 362-877. Oh, Mike, I got a call from Sergeant Mulcahey of the North Smithfield police looking for how to reach Bonnie Stevens. Something about telling her the two paints matched. Is she there?"

"Ed thanks a lot. I owe you for this, and I'll tell Bonnie the news," Mike answered as he hung up the phone.

"What news?" Bonnie asked.

"Goodman's truck paint matched the paint sample they took from your rental car in 1989. It looks like he's the guy who ran you off the road and nearly killed you."

"Son of a bitch, he's the same guy. Samantha, if you're right about him as Susan's killer, how do we get the bastard?" Bonnie yelled.

'Okay, okay, let's not get ahead of ourselves here. I've waited for a long time for something like this. Let's not screw it up by going off half-cocked. One step at a time," Mike replied.

At six on Saturday morning, the four had been up for an hour, had eaten breakfast, and were set to begin the surveillance outside the gated community. Alex had a pair of binoculars and positioned himself on the side of the car facing the entrance gate.

"Boy, I sure as heck hope Goodman's working on a Saturday. Otherwise, this may be a long day," he muttered.

At seven, cars were exiting the complex on a steady basis, but no Mercedes or Mazda. At seven-thirty, a black Mercedes scanned its card at the gate and the driver waved to the guard in the security station as he left.

"That's the car, Mike," Alex shouted excitedly.

"Okay, folks, just sit back and let's see where he's headed," Mike answered as he slowly pulled away from the roadside and began to follow the Mercedes, careful not to follow too closely, but close enough not to lose sight of the car.

After a ten minute ride on Route 192, the Mercedes made a right turn on Avalon Road. A half mile up the road was a building site where a condominium complex was being erected. Mike watched as the Mercedes pulled into the site and a rugged worker got out of the car, grabbed his construction helmet, and headed for a bulldozer on the property. His back was turned away from Mike's SUV as Samantha grabbed the binoculars from Alex's hands and focused on the guy.

"Come on, come on, damn it, turn around," she yelled. As he put the helmet on, the worker turned to return to his car as if he had forgotten something. Suddenly, there was dead silence. Everyone's eyes were on Samantha, waiting for some reaction.

"What do you see, Sammy, is it him?" shouted Alex.

"Look at the tattoo on his lower left arm. I can't make it out from here, but that face with a helmet on, he's the guy who's been in my dreams for years. I'm sure of it."

Mike quickly grabbed the binoculars and tried to focus on the arm tattoo, but their car was too far away for him to get a clear view. Goodman mounted the dozer and began to spread loam across the front of the complex.

Mike started the SUV and they pulled away from the work site.

"Let's go back to the entrance and see if this Martha Goodman comes out. Hopefully, we haven't missed her. She may be a way for us to get to the house when he's not home. I don't know if she works or not," he said.

It was nearly ten in the morning when they were back at the gated complex and parked across the street again. Alex expressed how sorry he was at not having his digital camera with the zoom lens. This would have at least allowed him to snap several shots of Goodman...even from a distance.

"How much do those cameras go for?" asked Mike.

"Probably five to six hundred with a zoom lens," Alex answered.

"We'll pick one up tonight. I didn't come this far to miss out on getting good shots of this guy if we need them," Mike added.

At one o'clock, just when they all started to get hungry, there appeared the red Miata sports car. A short-haired blonde, wearing sunglasses, pulled out from the gate and again they followed. The car pulled into a CVS lot and the woman went inside. They pulled the SUV in the same lot, but far enough away from the Miata so no one would notice them. Truth was most rental cars and vans in Florida are white. Their white SUV fit right in with the others in the lot. A red Mazda Miata convertible..... now that stood out.

The woman came out with a small bag, tossed it on the passenger seat, jumped in, and took off. Five minutes later, she pulled into the entrance to the Orlando Hills Country Club, another guard station facing them. This time, however, Mike followed. At the guard station, Mike expressed interest in becoming a member when asked why he was there. The guard wrote his name, the make and model of the rental, and the license plate number. He then handed Mike a set of directions to the entire complex, which included the golf course and connecting dining area, the tennis club, and an office where he could stop in to get information on residences in the complex.

"Did you see that red convertible that just went in ahead of us?" Mike asked with a smile. "Is she a resident?"

"No, she's not a resident. She's a tennis player. Plays every Saturday at this time. Her husband plays golf every Sunday," the guard eagerly replied.

"Thanks for your help. My wife and I, and my son and his wife, we're all interested in seeing what you've got here. I'll put that pass up here over the dashboard. Have a nice day."

Mike asked Bonnie which way the tennis club was, and they drove directly there after she located it on the property layout.

"Wow, these are nice courts," Samantha chimed in. "These are Har-Tru, the best hard court surface around. Gosh, there must be a dozen courts out there."

"How do you know so much about the courts, Samantha? Are you a tennis player?" Bonnie asked.

"I was on the high school tennis team back in
Hoboken, but I haven't played much since I've been at
Northeastern."

In a split second, Samantha opened the rear car door
on her side and stepped out.

"What are you doing, Samantha?" Mike asked.

"Nobody knows me. I'm just a girl interested in tennis
and maybe taking some lessons. I'll be right back."

Samantha walked toward the entrance to the pro shop
and locker area of the Laguna Tennis Club. Once inside,
she proceeded to the counter where a handsome young
man stood behind it.

"Hi, how can I help you?" the man asked.

"I'm new in Orlando, and I'm interested in taking a few
lessons to get my game back on track. It's been a while."

"Well, you've come to the right place. I'm Ted Morin.
I'm the head pro at Laguna and the guy you'd probably be
working with. Do you know your level as a player?"

"Yes, I'm a 3.5, but I haven't played in a couple of years."

"No problem, we can get you back to speed in no time.
Are you a member of the country club?"

"No, not yet. My husband and I just moved down here
from New Jersey. We just got out of school and he's taken a
job in the Orlando area.

"Okay. We can start you off with a few lessons, and if
you like the courts and the facility, we can talk about mem-
bership, leagues, and all that stuff later. Here's an application form with all the information you'll need. When do
you want to start?"

"I'm not sure just yet. We're still unpacking. Let me
get back to you on this. But can I get a tour of the place
first?"

"Sure, but I've got a lesson right now. You can roam around if you want to; maybe even watch the lesson from a distance if you choose to."

Samantha immediately made a bee line for the ladies locker room down the hallway near the members' lounge. As she entered the locker room, she heard the metal sound of a locker door closing only to come face to face with Marsha Goodman. She was dressed in a white tennis skirt and held a towel and tennis racquet in her hands. *This must be Morin's one-thirty lesson,* she thought.

"Hi, I'm Samantha Collins. I'm new here and thinking about taking lessons. Do you know the pro at the club?"

"Hello, I'm Marsha Goodman. I'm about to play with him right now. His name is Ted Morin, a real nice guy, and a great instructor. Have you met him?"

"Yes, I just did. He did tell me he had a lesson at one-thirty. Otherwise, he would have shown me around himself. My husband and I are looking for a place of our own, hopefully in a gated community if we can find one that's nice," Samantha answered. "I'm into tennis, he's into golf, and this place has both. We like the area and my husband just joined Stocktrade Securities as a broker. I have a teaching degree, so I'll be looking for some substitute position for now once we're settled in. There are so many private communities around; it's a bit confusing trying to narrow it down."

"Well, maybe I can help. My father is a builder and I was raised in the building industry all of my life," Marsha answered as she grabbed a business card for Pelican Homes from her purse in the locker, jotted down her home telephone number, and handed it to Samantha.

"Where are you staying?"

"We're at Windermere Estates for the week. After that, who knows?"

"Here is my telephone number. We live about ten minutes away from there. Give me a call tomorrow. Maybe I can get you to take a tour of Lakeview Terrace. I've got to go, can't keep Ted waiting. He charges by the hour, whether you're there or not."

Samantha strolled out of the tennis club back to the SUV holding the card with Marsha's phone number like the Statue of Liberty.

"Behold Marsha Goodman's home phone number. She wants me to call tomorrow to set us up for a tour of her housing community."

"So, what do we do now, Mr. Strange?" Bonnie asked.

CHAPTER 32

They left the golf course complex at two o'clock and headed back to the construction site on Avalon Road. At three, Zeke left the work site and headed for home. On Saturdays, he would normally return home from work, take a dip in the pool with a cocktail by his chair on the deck, and then shower, dress, and get ready to leave for the garage where the stolen car operation was run. The stolen cars were immediately prepared for resale out of Florida through fencing connections Zeke and his partner Danny Scott had developed over the years. They both were very careful at not being detected by anyone near the garage location.

Zeke left the house at four. He and Marsha hardly spoke, the way it normally was between the two of them.... a marriage of convenience. There was no sexual attraction between them, only occasional social appearances together at her father's invitation. Larry Pelican had no clue about the separate lives his daughter and son-in-law lived, nor would he have cared anyway, so long as the arrangement didn't embarrass his stature in the area.

As he left the gated community, Mike followed. The route was different and quickly led to more remote streets in Kissimmee. Mike kept his distance. He did not want to raise suspicion by Zeke. Ten minutes later, Zeke pulled up in front of a garage on a dead-end street. The large overhead door electronically opened and Zeke's Mercedes disappeared inside as the door closed behind him.

Bonnie noted the name over the door…Charlie's Tire and Auto Repair. Mike grabbed his cellphone, punched in the garage name in Kissimmee, and up popped the garage's telephone number. He entered the phone number and heard the ring at the other end of the line until a recording came on. "The number you have called, 378-1562, is no longer in service."

Bonnie used Alex's binoculars to get a close-up of the building. There were no windows in the front, so there wasn't much to see. Suddenly, the garage door started to open. A man dressed in jeans and a tee shirt stepped outside and looked down the road searching for movement in the area. He waved his hand forward like a cop directing traffic. Out came a black BMW58i, followed by a Lexus RS350 and a Cadillac Esplanade. They sped down the street and disappeared in less than a minute.

Bonnie shouted, "Mike, it's a chop shop. I'll bet these are all stolen cars. You would never see this many cars coming out of a repair shop all at once. Here comes another. Let me see if I can get the license plate number. Yes, it's JS-423, Florida plate on a silver Mercedes C250."

"I got it," Mike answered as he wrote the plate number on the back of a trash bag with empty coffee cups. He grabbed his cellphone again and called Ed Lemoine.

"Ed, we think Goodman might be running a stolen car business. We tailed him to a secluded garage and within ten minutes, four expensive cars came out all at once. We caught the license plate on the last one, a Mercedes C250, number JS-423, Florida plate. Can you work your magic again?"

"Hang on. Let me sign on to the Orlando police log and see what pops up."

Mike waited in silence as he could hear the sound of a keyboard punching keys rapidly.

"JS-423 is registered to a Philip Reed in Sanford. But it's a BMW58i, black, not a Mercedes. It was reported stolen at a supermarket yesterday morning. The car was being driven by a Carol Reed who reported it stolen around eleven in the morning on Friday."

"They're switching plates on the cars. Damn it, I wish we had a damn camera. We could have taken pictures of all four of them," Mike said.

"Time to call the local boys, Mike. You're getting too close to this guy and something is going to go wrong at some point," Lemoine answered.

"Not just yet, Ed. I don't have enough. What I don't need right now is for Goodman to get arrested on a lousy stolen car thing. I'm looking for making him pay for Susan and for Bonnie, the bastard. I'll get back to you."

"Bonnie, let's be sure we remember how to get back here if we need to. Get some landmarks and street names when we leave. Let's see if he goes back home from here."

Five minutes later, Zeke backed his car down the garage driveway and drove off as the garage door began to close.

The four of them slowly followed until Zeke pulled into a parking lot of the Kitty Lounge and went in. It was now nearly six o'clock and they were getting tired and hungry from the day's activity. Their day had started early that morning and as Mike pulled out of the nightclub's lot, Samantha spoke.

"I think I'll call Goodman's wife and see if she's still willing to give us a quick tour of her housing complex tomorrow. She said her husband plays golf on Sundays, so he wouldn't be around. Alex and I might be able to find out more about his schedule."

"That's a good idea," Mike said. "I think we'll need to rent another car in case Bonnie and I need to go out too. Let's do that after we get a bite. I'm starved. We can hit a Wal-Mart or something too and pick up a camera with a zoom lens. It would have been nice to have one today."

CHAPTER 33

Marsha Goodman was happy to give Samantha and Alex a tour of Lakeside Terrace on Sunday. They agreed to meet at her home at eleven. Marsha would alert the guards at the entrance of their arrival. They had rented a Toyota Corolla the night before and were ready to leave at ten-thirty on Sunday morning.

Homes at Lakeside Terrace were all built on a slab. Most builders in Florida never built foundations with basements. Storage and utilities were added either in a section of the garage or in a separate room off the kitchen. Marsha greeted them as they pulled into the Goodman driveway at 343 Lakeview Terrace. The sprawling one-level home had a huge open-spaced living room which led to a well-appointed dining room adjacent to the kitchen area. To the left of the kitchen was a cozy terrazzo-tiled family room, with sliders leading to a screened in-ground heated pool, complete with a Jacuzzi, and surrounded by a tiled patio area with several tables and umbrellas.

"Wow," Alex shouted. "This is beautiful. I bet the kids must use the pool a lot?"

"We don't have any children," Marsha responded with a disappointing look on her face. "It would be nice to have the company. My husband is not at home a lot. He works a lot."

"Oh, that's too bad. What does your husband do?" asked Samantha.

"He works for my father at Pelican Homes. He's some kind of a foreman there. And my father owns a nightclub on 192. Zeke keeps people in line at the club. It used to be only on Fridays and Saturdays, but now it's almost every night. Anyway, you didn't come here to listen to me whine about my married life, did you? Let's jump into our golf cart and I'll show you around the complex. It's quite nice."

She drove them through several streets of similar homes to a community center where there was an arcade, an events room complete with kitchen, and an exercise room filled with equipment. A sauna and shower facility was tucked just off the exercise area. Marsha then drove them to the management office. She had informed the office she would be bringing guests over to get more information on available homes for sale. All of this took about an hour and a half and they returned to her home. Samantha and Alex thanked her for her hospitality and left.

They had agreed to meet back at the rental house for lunch and to determine their next move. Alex mentioned how Goodman worked practically every night at the Kitty Lounge and how Samantha and him might drop in on Sunday night to get a close-up of Goodman. Mike and Bonnie would return to Charlie's Tire and Auto Repair armed with their new zoom-lensed digital camera to see if there was more activity going on. This time they would position the SUV to get clear shots of any vehicles exiting the garage, but far enough away to stay undetected. From three to six that afternoon, there was no activity near the garage site and they decided to head back to their rental house.

After a quick pizza and wine take-out at the house, Samantha and Alex rose to go to the Kitty Lounge.

"I don't like the idea of just the two of you doing this without us being somewhere in the area," Mike said. "Suppose something goes wrong. I can't think of what at the moment, but I'd feel better if we tagged along. We can stay in the SUV until you come out. If for some reason you don't come out within an hour, we'll come in ourselves to find you."

The four of them were quiet in the car as they approached the nightclub. Samantha was about to come face to face with the nightmare in her dreams, and she just didn't have any idea how she would react. Alex held her hand as they walked toward the entrance. Once inside, the glaring lights shone on a stage with half-naked pole dancers, waitresses paraded back and forth barely clothed in mini-aprons carrying trays of drinks from the bar, and music blaring much too loudly. They slowly made their way to the bar, popped themselves up on stools, and ordered martinis. Within a minute, Zeke Goodman appeared to the right of them at the corner of the bar. He was having a conversation with the bartender as Samantha stared at him through the mirror facing her behind the bar.

"Oh, my God," she sighed. "Put a worker's helmet on this guy and he's the guy in my dreams. Alex, I'm getting nervous just looking at him. Let's go. I've seen what I came here to see."

Mike was surprised to see the two of them walking back to the car so soon after they had gone in to the club.

"I can't look at him anymore. He scares me. Can we leave please?"

* * *

On Monday morning, Zeke arrived at the work site and headed for the bulldozer nearby. As he climbed on, he noticed an envelope on the seat. He opened it and read the contents from a single folded sheet of paper. *You should have finished the job in Cumberland in 1989.*

He looked around the condominium worksite and all he could see were other Pelican workers, no one else. He put the paper back in the envelope, placed it in the pocket of his jacket, a worried look on his face. He had all but forgotten about anything involving his brother-in-law. In the last twenty years, he had done very well for himself, had no intention of returning to Rhode Island, and wondered what suddenly came up to remind him of the two incidences from his past.

At three, he left in his Mercedes and headed home. As he entered the house, he spotted a note from Marsha that she was at the neighbor's house and would be back at four. Next to the note was Monday's mail in a small pile on the kitchen counter. Zeke thumbed through the usual ads, circulars, and utility bills until, at the bottom of the pile, there was another white envelope simply addressed to Zeke

Goodman in printed block letters. He eyed the envelope and cautiously began to open it. Again, inside was a single sheet of folded paper with the words, *A* few *bullets in my body won't kill me. Who am I?*

When Marsha came in at four, she found Zeke sitting by the pool, staring blankly at the water and holding a drink in his hand.

"You okay?" she asked.

"The mail today, was it all in the mailbox?" he asked very slowly.

"Yes, it was. There was one envelope though with just your name on it, no address. What was that?" she asked.

"Just Andy down the street with a name of a friend of his looking for a job. I may have something for him," Zeke replied sheepishly.

"Well, aren't we Mr. Wonderful all of a sudden."

"What's that supposed to mean? I think you're pretty well taken care of, and I don't bother you too often, do I?"

"We don't have much of a life together, Zeke. You're off early in the morning, take a dip in the afternoon with a cocktail, then I don't see you the rest of the night until eleven or later. You're either at the club or somewhere else, but not with me. What kind of a marriage is that?"

"Marsha, I told your father I would take care of you, and I'm doing what I promised. I've got a lot on my mind right now and I don't need to listen to your whining. Anytime you want to end the agreement, it's fine with me. I am what I am, and if it's not good enough for you, go back to daddy anytime. So back off, I've got to go out right now."

"So what else is new? Someday, Zeke, you'll wish you were nicer to me. There'll be a day when you need me and I won't be there. So, go ahead, go out and play your foolish games with women from the club, or whatever it is you spend your nights doing. Because one night, you'll come home and I won't be here anymore," Marsha answered as she entered the house and shut the sliding glass door behind her.

He entered the house from a separate slider off the bedroom. He showered, dressed, and left the house without even acknowledging Marsha's presence. She sat in the family room, TV turned on, with tears rolling down her cheeks as he left.

Zeke was not aware of the SUV following him from a distance. He was on his way to the garage. The weekend had been very busy. Ten cars had been stolen on Saturday and Sunday, and they had to be moved quickly out of Florida within a day. His buyer from Georgia expected all ten vehicles by late Monday night. Zeke's cut from Danny Scott would be nearly five thousand dollars for fencing these cars. Most of the money Zeke had stashed in a wall safe behind a picture in his bedroom. Even Marsha did not know the combination to the safe.

All ten cars were considered high-end luxury cars. The license plates were switched, and a false registration was drawn up to match the plates. And all other owner information was removed and tossed in trash barrels in the garage. Once a week, the trash barrels were taken behind the garage and all the information was burned. Over the years, they had been very cautious in this operation.

Mike parked the SUV in an unsuspecting spot far away from the garage. He then walked toward a wooded area that faced the garage door, but still at a safe distance. One by one, he snapped photo after photo of each car as it left the garage at five in the afternoon. As Zeke exited the garage afterwards, Mike snapped several shots of him driving away. Bonnie waved to Mike from the SUV and drove it slowly toward the garage as Mike emerged from the wooded area and walked directly toward the garage door. He taped a white envelope to the door. The envelope was addressed to Zeke Goodman.

CHAPTER 34

"We've got a problem," the voice on the phone began.

"What problem?" asked Zeke on Monday afternoon as he answered his cellphone from the seat in his bulldozer.

"I just came from Charlie's and there was an envelope taped to the garage door with your name on it," answered Danny Scott. "Who else even knows about the garage?"

"Nobody knows. You have no idea how careful I am when I go there," Zeke answered smugly.

"Well, somebody knows, Zeke, and now we've got to move the operation after all these years. Damn it, Zeke, I told you to make sure no one was following you. No new deals for a while. We can't risk it. If nothing happens, we can start up again. I'll start looking for another spot."

"And I'm telling you, Danny, I've never seen a car within five hundred feet of the garage."

"Not good enough today. With the scopes people have today, they can follow you from a thousand yards away. Find out who this is, Zeke, and do it now. What do you want me to do with this envelope?"

"Leave it inside the garage on the desk. I'll be there in an hour or so. And, if somebody is following me, you don't want to be anywhere close to the garage when I get there. I'll find out what's going on. Trust me, Danny, I don't know what this is all about, but I'll let you know when I have more," Zeke emphasized.

After he ended the call, he turned off the motor to the bulldozer, jumped to the ground below, and bolted for his car. As he left the construction site, he scrutinized all cars behind him as he drove toward the garage using a different series of roads. All he noticed was a white van several hundred yards behind him which appeared to make all the same turns he did. But as he neared the garage, there were no vehicles anywhere near the dead-end street.

He entered the garage, closed the overhead door, and rushed to the desk in the far corner. There sat the third envelope he had received in as many days. He quickly opened the unsealed envelope and read the message on a folded single sheet of paper.

You can run a car off the road, but your old pickup truck just gave you away. I'm coming for you.

Zeke was furious. He swiped his hand across the desk, knocking everything to the floor. He then picked up the desk chair and flung it across the garage floor. Then he exited from a back door to the garage and walked toward a wooded area to the right of the building. He followed the tree line along the street toward the first connecting street down the road. Mike spotted his movement and began to run furiously back to the SUV where Bonnie sat with the camera. Mike yelled at her to start the car. He jumped in on the passenger side and they sped off quickly. Zeke caught a glimpse of the vehicle and noted the first three numbers of the license plate before it was out of range.

"Step on it, Bonnie. He came around the building through the woods. There must be a back door to the garage. If he got the plate number, it's only a matter of time before he finds out the car was rented to me. We're going to have to move faster to get this guy before he gets the plate information. We can't assume he didn't get the plate number," Mike said.

"And the note we just left about hitting my car, he has to remember I worked for you on the radon case. This was the whole point of running me off the road," Bonnie added.

"Let's get back to the house and talk to Samantha and Alex," Mike added. "I've got an idea." He grabbed his cell-phone and punched in a number off his speed dial list.

"Ed, can you get away and come down to Orlando for a day or two? He knows we're on to him now and we could use your help with the local boys here in Orlando. I don't know how we can get the Orlando police involved except on the stolen car business. But I think their garage will be empty by the time the police get there anyway."

"Give me your address in Orlando. I'll be on the next plane down there. In the meantime, buy some food at the market, and stay put after that until I get there. Understood?"

"Understood."

The Corolla had not been seen by Zeke at any time. Samantha and Alex had one last visit planned on Monday night at the Kitty Lounge. They would enter the club at eight o'clock, check to see if Goodman was there, casually nurse a drink at the bar, and then Samantha would leave the club ahead of Alex. While he kept an eye on Goodman in the club, she would locate Goodman's Mercedes and slip an envelope under the driver's side windshield wipers. Alex would follow shortly after, and they would return to the rental house.

Ed Lemoine's flight from Providence on Southwest arrived in Orlando on time. He was met at the airport by Detective Ron Gardner of the Orlando Police Department at seven-thirty. Lemoine and Gardner had served on the same drug trafficking task force in Providence in early 2010. Gardner's team in Orlando had traced drug shipments from Orlando to Providence on a yacht docked at the Apponaug Harbor Marina in Warwick. Lemoine's assignment to the task force had occurred because of his successful drug raids in the Cumberland/Pawtucket area. There was speculation of a leak in the Providence Police Department, and the DEA wanted an outsider on the team, and Lemoine was perfect for the job. Gardner appreciated the help on the case and had told Lemoine he hoped to someday repay him for his participation on the case.

When Lemoine called Gardner early that afternoon, he indicated a twenty-year-old cold case had been re-opened, and a prime suspect had been traced to the Orlando area. Lemoine said he would land in Orlando early in the evening, and the victims who had found the perpetrator needed local help. Gardner agreed to help in any way he could.

They left the airport in Gardner's car and took Route 4 toward Windermere Estates. Mike had left word at the guard station of Lemoine's anticipated arrival. Both detectives arrived at the rental house at eight-fifteen, five minutes after Samantha and Alex had returned.

Gardner was introduced to the two couples and was briefed on the breakthrough in the case involving Goodman.

"How in the world did you two even ask about Goodman in the first place?" Gardner asked as he faced Samantha and Alex.

"Well, the only logical assumption led to the building contractor or someone affiliated with him. Goodman, it turns out, is the brother-in-law of the contractor in the radon gas case. Nobody thought to question him because he was nowhere to be found after the murder. Supposedly, he had moved to Florida months before, but that turned out to be a lie by the contractor. When I mentioned this to Mike and Bonnie, one thing led to another. Paint chips from his old truck were matched with paint found on the rear end of Bonnie's car when she was run off the road in 1989 while working on the radon case. Goodman tried to cover this up when he had his truck painted right after the incident," Samantha answered.

"But why are you here? I can understand Mike and Bonnie being directly involved. It's his wife we're talking about, and it's Bonnie who he tried to kill by running her off the road," Gardner asked.

"If I told you, you wouldn't believe me. Let's just say I need to see this through. This woman's murder has to be solved and now that I'm into this, I want to see it done."

"This is dangerous business you're messing around with here. If this is all true, the murder, running Bonnie off the road, and the car theft ring, this guy could easily eliminate his problems by eliminating all of you. You're putting the squeeze on a potentially very dangerous man. And you still haven't told me how you connect this Goodman guy to the murder of your wife, Mr. Strange. I can see the evidence linking him to Bonnie's case, but how does this make him a murderer?"

"Trust us on this, Detective. We just know he's the one. And we've set a trap for him later tonight," Mike answered.

"What are you talking about?"

"We've been leaving unsigned notes addressed to him at his house, on the seat of his bulldozer at work, on the garage door of the stolen car spot, and just now on the windshield of his car at the Kitty Lounge. This last one should draw him out for sure," Mike went on.

"I thought we agreed you would all stay put until I got here, Mike," Lemoine barked. "This is how people get hurt, when they don't realize what they're doing. God damn it, Mike, what kind of notes are we talking about here?"

"The last one Samantha and Alex just dropped off at the nightclub gave Goodman an ultimatum, *Bring a half million dollars to the guard station at Windermere Estates by eleven o'clock tonight. Put it in a plastic bag and put the bag in a sealed box addressed to Susan Strange. Then turn around and leave. You'll never hear from me again. The next time you try to shoot someone, make sure you finish the job.* We included a photo of Susan with the note."

"That's your plan. You people have been watching too much TV," echoed Gardner.

"No one knows Ed down here. What if he takes the place of the guard on duty around nine o'clock? We know there are security cameras watching every car coming and going, so we can record the drop off," Mike said.

"Jesus, guys, this doesn't prove anything. What note? Do you think Goodman will admit any wrongdoing here, based on what? He'll just say he was paid $100 to drop off a box on his way home by some guy at the nightclub. Why not an easy $100? Call him up at the club right now and tell him there's been a change of plans and you'll call him back. Here, use my cellphone. It's untraceable, but it'll record all conversations on it."

"I don't know what the hell you people think you're doing. Ed, what's really going on here?" Gardner yelled.

"I don't know, Ron, I really don't know. What is it you're not telling me about Goodman? Why do I get the feeling you're holding something back from me, Mike?" Lemoine asked.

Mike glanced at Samantha who realized her secret had to be revealed. *Another two people to convince that I'm not crazy,* she pondered. Ed noticed the focus on Samantha and looked at her with a shoulder shrug.

"Okay, what's going on? Young lady, your little innocent coverage for a college newspaper sounds kind of lame right about now," Ed blurted as he questioned Samantha.

"I can tell you for sure Samantha's done nothing wrong," Alex chimed in.

"Spoken like a true boyfriend," Lemoine retorted.

"Stop it, please, no more. Will this ever stop controlling my life?" Samantha yelled. "I'll tell you everything, but you won't believe me. I don't care anymore. I found this guy and he's real, and exactly what I said he was."

Bonnie made the call posing as Susan Strange. Zeke started swearing on the other end of the phone and yelled threats of payback once he found out who she said she was. Gardner listened to the threats and realized there likely was some truth to what they all had been saying about Goodman.

"Okay, Samantha, why are you really here?"

CHAPTER 35

Over the next hour, Samantha watched the looks on the faces of Ed Lemoine and Ron Gardner as she related her childhood nightmares and the developments which led to the current revelations to Mike and Bonnie earlier in the week. Ironically, neither of them thought Samantha was crazy. They both equated her experiences as similar to a medium who could speak to the dead and relate conversations to a living relative or friend. In certain cases, police departments in various parts of the country ask assistance from these gifted people, often with a good deal of success.

However, neither Lemoine nor Gardner had dealt with someone who claimed she had a life before her own. Both had heard of the Indian belief of reincarnation, but not to the level Samantha related to them. Lemoine now could understand her curiosity with the mysterious and elusive Zeke Goodman, the brother-in-law who conveniently disappeared before anyone knew he even really existed. Goodman had been right under the nose of the Cumberland police all along, and Lemoine felt a sense of failure on his part for the omission after all these years.

"I can understand why this wouldn't fly in a courtroom," Lemoine began. "No judge or jury would ever believe any of this about your wife's murder, Mike. There's enough evidence and motive on Bonnie's hit and run, but Samantha testifying at a murder trial would be a field day for the defense. No, we've got to get this guy some other way."

"You mean you actually believe me?" Samantha asked.

"Samantha, I don't know you at all," Gardner said. "But there's no way you could have made this up. There are so many details you know about Susan Strange, her house, her husband, the actual murder, and the description of the guy who did it, there's too much factual information no one could deny. And I'm guessing if we give you enough time, you'd probably remember even more. I'm wondering about the random detour which took you through Cumberland. The Phantom Farm sign and then Burke Road, this seems like it was meant to be. Did you ever think this would ever come out this way?"

"Mr. Gardner, you earlier asked me what I was doing in Orlando. Do you still wonder why I'm here?" she asked.

"Mike and I felt the same way," Bonnie chimed in. "The things she knew about Mike and about Goodman, no one else could have told her this. She was just a baby when this happened over twenty-two years ago. We can't let this go without seeing it through. It's tormented Mike since 1989, and me too. And I can just imagine what's going through Samantha's head these days."

"The only way we'll get this guy is by getting his confession on video. There were no witnesses, no evidence trail, and no prior attempts by Goodman as far as the records show. What about Tate?" asked Lemoine. "If he lied about Goodman being around at the time of the murder, he must be involved. Maybe we can get him to tell us more. What if we tell him Goodman is under arrest in Florida and confessed about the murder and implicated Tate as knowing all about it? Maybe Tate told Goodman to take off before someone questioned him, or maybe Tate paid him to do these things."

"Ron, if we spook Tate too soon and he doesn't bite, he may alert Goodman, and I wouldn't be surprised if Goodman disappears real quickly," added Lemoine. "The main focus has to be on Goodman. We can go after Tate once we get Goodman. The question is, how do we get this guy?"

"Let's see how Goodman is when Ed and I pay him a visit tomorrow at his work site," Gardner said.

Lemoine had booked a room at a nearby Econolodge and he and Gardner instructed the two couples not to leave the complex until they returned from their questioning of Goodman.

The following morning at eight o'clock, Gardner picked up Lemoine in the breakfast area of the hotel. They would set the stage for their visit to Goodman by first visiting his wife at their home. As they arrived at Lakeview Terrace, Lemoine rang the doorbell.

"Mrs. Goodman? Is your husband at home?" asked Gardner as he flashed his badge for the Orlando police. "I'm Lieutenant Gardner from the Orlando PD, and this is Detective Lemoine from the Cumberland, Rhode Island police."

"No, Zeke left about a half hour ago. What's this about?" she asked.

"Just some routine questions, ma'am. It's about an old case in Cumberland some twenty years ago that your husband might be able to help us with," Lemoine answered.

"Oh, wow, long before I met him. He should be at the construction site on Avalon Road off 192 until three."

The two detectives thanked Marsha Goodman and left the house. No sooner were they out of the driveway, Marsha picked up the telephone and called Zeke on his cellphone.

"Zeke, were you involved in something when you were living in Rhode Island?" she asked.

"What the hell are you talking about?" he asked.

"A couple of detectives, one from the Orlando police and the other from Cumberland, Rhode Island were just here looking for you. They said it had to do with an old case in Rhode Island over twenty years ago."

"What did you tell them?"

"I told them they could find you at work on Avalon Road. What's this all about?"

"I don't know. If they come here, I'll find out, I guess," Zeke answered with a worried sound in his voice.

At nine o'clock, Lemoine and Gardner pulled up in front of the condo site and asked a worker where they could find Zeke Goodman. As they approached the bull-dozer Zeke was operating, he turned off the motor and jumped down off the vehicle to greet them.

"Can I help you?" he asked.

After they introduced themselves to Zeke, Lemoine began.

"Mr. Goodman, were you working for Tate Builders in the summer of 1989?"

"Only in late spring, that's the year I moved down here to work for Pelican. I've been with them ever since. Why do you ask?"

"We're just following up on a cold case in Cumberland about that time and your name was in the file. A young woman was murdered in her home back then and you and Jonathan Tate were mentioned in the file."

"I'm afraid I can't help you there. I don't know anything about a murder. Why would someone shoot a young woman anyway? I was in Orlando in July, 1989. You said my brother-in-law was also mentioned?"

"Yes, his company was being sued by some condo owners for radon exposure and the woman who was murdered was the wife of the lawyer handling the lawsuit against Tate."

"I did hear about the law suit from Jonathan at some point late in the summer. But what's that got to do with me? I drove a dozer for the company, and when he told me the law suit had been settled early the following year, I was happy for him. I don't see him or my sister too often. They're not Florida travelers, and I haven't been north since I left in 1989. Why was my name in your file on this?"

"Probably because Tate is your brother-in-law and you've got a record, Mr. Goodman. Mr. Strange still believes the Tates had something to do with his wife's death," answered Lemoine.

"So you were in Florida when the murder occurred?"

"If there had been a murder when I was there, I would have remembered it, detective. But since I wasn't in Rhode Island, this is the first I hear about it. What did you say the name of the woman was?" asked Zeke.

"I didn't. But her name was Susan Strange. Why do you ask?"

"I thought maybe I'd recognize the name from when I lived there. But no, the name doesn't ring a bell. And as far as my record goes, I haven't had as much as a parking ticket in the last twenty years. The Zeke Goodman you're talking about doesn't exist anymore."

"We'd appreciate it if you would stick around the Orlando area for a few weeks in case we need to ask you some more questions," Gardner stated.

"Not a problem, I'm not going anywhere."

As the two detectives left the construction site, they didn't notice the black BMW parked across the road. Danny Scott sat there until they left, and then followed the car until it turned into Windermere Estates. Goodman's meeting with the two detectives did not sit lightly with Scott. He would confront Zeke about the meeting. Too many things were happening all of a sudden to threaten his lucrative stolen car business.

"How did it go with Goodman?" asked Mike as they entered the rental house.

"He knew we were coming. We visited his wife first at their house and she must have called him at work. This guy was too accommodating," Lemoine said as he pulled out his notebook.

"He said he was in Orlando in July, 1989 and knew nothing about a murder. Funny thing though, I never told him when the murder happened. So why would he tell me he was in Orlando in July of that year?"

"But this is not true, Ed. We have employment records from Tate which show Goodman still working there until the fifteenth of July. I'll bet if you check Pelican's records, he didn't start there until sometime in August," Mike said.

"And get this, folks. He wondered why anyone would shoot a young woman. We never told him Susan was shot, we just said murdered."

"Ed, let's bring him in for more questioning. I want to rattle this guy's cage. We haven't even mentioned the stolen car business yet, or the attempted murder on Bonnie with his pick-up truck," Gardner added.

At two o'clock on the same day, they were back on Avalon Road. Zeke saw them coming, and this time wasn't as pleasant as earlier in the day.

"What's on your mind this time, detective?"

"We'd like you to come down to the station for some more questions. We've got some things there you might be able to help us with. It would be very helpful to us."

"And if I say no, what then?" asked Goodman with a disdainful look on his face.

"I'm afraid we might not ask so nicely. Since you obviously have nothing to hide, I'm sure you won't have a problem with coming in. This shouldn't take long," Gardner answered. "You can follow us in your car if you want."

"Okay, okay, but I don't get off here until three. How about I meet you there?"

"Not a problem for us to wait until three. We're looking forward to your help."

CHAPTER 36

The ride from Avalon Road to the Raleigh Street station in Orlando took about twenty minutes. Ron Gardner drove his car slow enough to keep a constant eye in his rear-view mirror to be certain Goodman's black Mercedes was not too far behind. The twenty minutes to the station allowed the detectives time to line up their questioning to Goodman when they arrived.

As Goodman entered the police station, he had more than a worried look on his face. Gardner led the way to a second floor interrogation room, complete with two-way mirror. These mirrors were all too common in police interrogation rooms. Danny Scott had followed Goodman and was visibly upset when Goodman entered the station with two detectives. All he could think about was *what's Zeke doing with two cops at this station? Do I smell a rat?* He decided to wait to see how long Zeke would be there. Once he came out of the station, he would call him on his cellphone to ask if anything further was happening following the note left at Charlie's garage. Zeke's answer would tell him whether he was lying to him or not.

Meanwhile, inside the interrogation room, Gardner asked Goodman to have a seat. Lemoine stood with his back to the wall behind Gardner.

"Mr. Goodman, what can you tell us about Charlie's Tire and Auto Repair?" asked Gardner.

"Never heard of the place."

"Really! This is odd. Isn't this you coming out of the garage yesterday afternoon?"

Gardner slipped an eight by ten color photo of Goodman at the wheel of his Mercedes with the garage's name sign in the background.

"Oh, is that the name of the garage? I was losing tire pressure in my left rear tire yesterday after work and one of the guys said this guy was good with tires. So I had him fix it."

"You wouldn't have a receipt from the garage would you?"

"For a bum tire, what for? I paid him cash anyway."

"Then you wouldn't know anything about all of these cars leaving the garage just before you?" Gardner continued as he placed several photos in a row on the table in front of Goodman.

"I guess he does a good tire business."

"All of these cars were reported stolen a day earlier, Mr. Goodman."

"You mean this guy doesn't just sell tires and stuff?" Goodman asked with a smirk on his face.

"But you don't know anything about this business, do you?"

"Hey, wait a minute here. Is this why I'm here, because you thought I was involved with this guy stealing cars?" Goodman asked with a raised voice.

"I don't believe we ever said anything of the kind. Your picture was taken right after these cars left the garage and we're just trying to find out what you were doing there."

Ed Lemoine stepped forward and asked, "Right about this time, you should be wondering, *what does a detective from Cumberland, Rhode Island have to do with all of this?* At least, I would be wondering if I were you."

"I'm assuming you're here about the murder up there in 1989. I told you, I know nothing about a murder."

"Yes, I remember, you did tell us this morning. As a matter of fact, Mr. Goodman," Lemoine stated as he thumbed through his note pad, "you said you wondered who would shoot such a young woman. But you see, Mr. Goodman, we never said the woman was shot. All we said was she was murdered."

"I just assumed she was shot," Goodman meekly replied, sweat visibly accumulating on his forehead.

"You also stated you weren't in the area at the time and date of the murder. You mentioned you had already left for Orlando. Is this correct?"

"Yes, that's true."

"Well, Mr. Goodman, we have proof you were still working for Tate Builders at the time and you didn't leave for Orlando until late July of '89."

"I could be wrong on the exact date. Heck, this was over twenty-two years ago. So what?"

"So unless you were living under a rock, you had to have known or heard about the murder. It was the biggest news in the area."

"I don't remember," Goodman stuttered. "Am I going to need a lawyer here?" he asked.

"This is up to you, Mr. Goodman. Do you feel you need to have a lawyer before we continue?" asked Lemoine.

"Sounds to me like your old case needs someone to blame for the murder, and because I've got a record, I'm an easy target."

"Why would Jonathan Tate back then state you weren't around at the time, when you really were?"

"I don't know. You'll have to ask him that question."

"We will, Mr. Goodman, we will. We've got just a few more questions. We're almost done for today."

The questioning was clearly upsetting Goodman and his replies did not sound very creditable. He did not pursue any attempt to call a lawyer. The truth was, he had not dealt with any lawyer since the closing on his Lake Terrace property several years earlier. A real estate lawyer would not have been his first choice at the moment.

"Does the name Bonnie Stevens mean anything to you, Mr. Goodman?"

"I don't know the name at all," he answered.

"When you were in Rhode Island, did you own a blue Ford pickup truck?"

"Yes, I did. I sold it back to the guy I bought it from right before I moved down here. I needed the money for the move."

"Would the guy you dealt with be Frank Mohan in Bellingham?"

"Yes, he's the guy. Wow, that's a long time ago. Is he still around?"

"Oh, yes, he's very much still around. Sharp as a tack, and keeps very meticulous records of all his transactions. Especially the black paint job and bumper repair on the truck in July, 1989."

"I can't say I remember this, but it's possible."

"And don't you know, the truck is still used by Mohan's nephew to plow his driveway at his place in New Hampshire."

"What's your point, detective? What's the old truck got to do with anything?"

"Bonnie Stevens was a paralegal for Mike Strange, the husband of the murdered woman we talked about earlier. Her car was run off the road in North Smithfield by a blue pickup truck. Bonnie nearly died from the crash, Mr. Goodman. And, do you know what? The paint chips off her car's rear end match exactly to the blue paint underneath your repainted black truck."

"That's it. Now I'm supposed to have rammed a car off the road twenty-two years ago. Do you know how many blue pickup trucks there were back then? Everyone had a blue pickup."

"But not everyone had a blue pickup with a dent in the bumper from a head-on crash, I'll bet?" Lemoine responded.

"I want a lawyer," Goodman shouted.

"No need of a lawyer for now, Mr. Goodman. You're free to go, but please stay in the area," Gardner stated.

Goodman rose from his seat, pushed his chair back hard until it toppled over, and rushed out the door of the interrogation room, down the stairs and out the front door. He had been there for thirty minutes and was relieved to be outside. No sooner did he start his car, his cellphone rang.

"Danny, what's up?" Goodman asked.

"Just following up on the note at the garage, Zeke. Did you find out who it was from?" asked Danny Scott.

"I've got it under control, Danny, but no sense in taking chances. It would be safer to move elsewhere just to be sure. You agree?"

"Absolutely. We wouldn't want the police closing in on us or anything like that, would we?"

"I don't think the cops down here have a clue of what we're doing. I don't like to even be in the same room with a cop, if you know what I mean?"

"Zeke, I hear what you're saying. You couldn't catch me either with any of them. I don't trust them," said Scott.

"I'll call you back when we're all set up again. Spend some time with your wife. You never know how long you'll be together," he said. Danny Scott was not a happy man at the moment.

CHAPTER 37

Zeke walked in the house through the door in the garage. Marsha noticed the Mercedes in the garage as he entered and found it quite strange.

"What's going on, Zeke? Are you okay? You never park your car in the garage until you get home from the club."

"I'm not going to the club tonight. I'm staying home. What's for dinner?" he asked without even stopping his walk to the bedroom. "I'm going for a swim."

Marsha stood there with her mouth open, trying to understand what had just happened. Zeke had not eaten dinner at home in several months, preferring to pick up something on his way to the club around six each night. The only time he and Marsha ate dinner together was at some event or function put on by her father Larry for a building association. You couldn't really call this a quiet dinner for two since the events were always tables of eight people or more. She was at a loss for words on a dinner choice. She walked in the bedroom and found Zeke naked as he reached for his bathing suit hanging on a drying rack nearby.

"Oops, sorry for barging in, but are you feeling okay? I feel like I'm dealing with a perfect stranger here."

"I've had a tough day. I just left the police station where two detectives questioned me about a stolen car ring operation here in Orlando, and then they tried to implicate me in a murder and attempted murder in Rhode Island over twenty years ago. So, spare me the wisecracks."

"Listen, asshole, you want to treat me like I'm your waitress, then make your own dinner. You know why, because I don't even remember what you like to eat anyway, it's been so long. Enjoy your swim, and be careful not to hit your head on the bottom of the pool when you dive. The pool guy just cleaned it this morning before we had sex on the patio."

"You gotta be a smart ass all the time, don't you? You've been a spoiled daddy's girl all your life. You don't know what it's like to have to work to make a living, do you? Daddy isn't the one who bought this place, is he? And he's not the one who lets you drive around in your little convertible screwing around all day. How's your tennis game these days? You talk about me with some of the girls at the club. You think I don't know about your extra activities with Ted Morin? Everybody at the club knows what's going on after your tennis lessons. So spare me the bullshit and work on something for supper."

"What the hell are you involved in now, Zeke? Why are the cops after you? And what's this stuff about Rhode Island twenty years ago?"

"Nothing I can't handle, and certainly nothing which involves you. I'll handle it."

As Marsha turned to go back into the kitchen, she noticed a gun on his nightstand. She knew Zeke had bought one several years back for protection in case someone broke into the house, but she had not seen the gun for years. The sight of the gun in plain view made her nervous and she questioned him on it.

"What's this for?"

"Just being careful. I had to throw a couple of drunks out of the nightclub yesterday, and they sort of threatened to get even. You never know about guys like this."

"Really? Have you looked in the mirror lately? You can't soar with eagles, you know, when you deal with assholes."

"Yea, well, those assholes are what I have to deal with all the time so you can play in your castle all day or at your tennis club."

She stormed out of the bedroom into the kitchen area and reached for the open bottle of cabernet. She poured herself a tall glass and began to drink. The wine calmed her down as she could see Zeke near the pool through the sliders in the kitchen. *Why do I stay with this guy?* she wondered. *I can do better for myself than this.* Her thoughts were suddenly interrupted by the phone ringing.

"I'd like to speak to Zeke Goodman, please."

"Who is this?" Marsha asked.

"His worst nightmare, sweetie," the female voice on the other end of the receiver said.

"Does this nightmare have a name, dearie?" Marsha asked sarcastically.

"Just tell him it's Susan Strange from Cumberland, and I'm back in the game after a long absence. I'm at Windermere."

Marsha walked to the pool patio and left the phone on one of the tables near the pool steps. She turned to Zeke and said.

"It's someone named Susan from Cumberland. She said she was back in the game."

Zeke's face dropped as he wiped the water away from his eyes. He reached for the phone and all he could hear was a dial tone.

"Marsha, did you give out this number to anyone? We have an unlisted number, and no one calls it except for your father and Karen next door?"

"No, I don't remember giving it out to anyone. I use my cellphone most of the time anyway."

As she walked back into the kitchen, she did remember writing her telephone number on the back of a Pelican Builders business card for the young woman at the tennis club. She thought to herself, *what was her name?* Suddenly, she remembered.....Samantha Collins. She then recalled they were staying at Windermere Estates. She reached for her cellphone and punched in the number for Windermere after finding it in her phonebook. She asked to be connected to the guard station.

"My friend, Samantha Collins, I believe is staying in one of the units this week. Is there some way you can verify this for me?" she asked.

"No, I don't have anyone by the name of Collins registered."

"Oh, she must be there. She's about in her early twenties, brown hair, with her husband Alex. They were driving a Toyota Corolla."

"Oh, that's the Strange residence, Michael Strange. The young couple just registered the rental car so they could get a gate pass. They're in 2305 Cranmore.

"Zeke, does the name Michael Strange mean anything to you?" Marsha asked as she yelled from the open sliders.

"Yea, he was the lawyer who handled a law suit against Jonathan a long time ago. Why?"

"I just remembered giving out our number to a young woman I met a couple of days ago at the tennis club. She called on Saturday, and I gave her and her husband a tour of Lakeview Terrace on Sunday. Apparently, they just moved to Orlando and were looking for a place down here."

"So you just decided to be their tour guide. This is why we have a management office, Marsha, so residents don't have to bother. What does this have to do with Michael Strange?"

"I remember they said they were staying at Windermere this week, so I called to find out if they were still there. Apparently they're staying in a unit with Michael Strange, 2305 Cranmore."

"What did you say their names were?"

"Alex and Samantha Collins."

"I never heard of them," Zeke answered.

"Maybe they're here with the Stranges."

"What do you mean the Stranges?"

"Michael and Susan Strange, the woman who just called."

* * *

The stage was set. The video cameras had been hidden in the living room ceiling vent, above the cabinets in the corner of the kitchen, and out by the pool area. The monitors were in one of the upstairs bedrooms where Lemoine sat in the dark. In the kitchen, Mike and Bonnie, and Samantha and Alex, pretended to be playing a card game as they sat at a high top table near the slid-ers leading to the pool area. It was after eight o'clock and getting dark. Meanwhile, Ron Gardner was positioned in the corner of the guard station with his eyes focused on any vehicles entering the complex. There was no assur-ance Goodman would appear this night, but Bonnie's ear-lier phone call to the Goodman house, posing as Susan Strange, would hopefully arouse Goodman's curiosity. Marsha's inquiry at the guard station earlier had been passed on to Gardner.

At eight-thirty, Zeke threw on a shirt over a pair of shorts and Marsha heard the garage door open. Before she could get to the garage, she heard Zeke's car backing out of the driveway, and the garage door closing behind him. She wondered where he was off to, but hurried to the bed-room. The gun on the nightstand was no longer there.

Zeke grabbed his cellphone and called Ernie Brady, another bouncer at the Kitty Lounge.

"Ernie, this is Zeke. I need to stop by for a minute tonight. I'm right around the corner from Windermere. How do I get past the guard station? Are you still at 1200 Dawes?"

"No problem, Zeke. I'll call them and they'll let you in. Anything I need to know?"

"No, I might need to change your schedule next week, and I thought we'd just look at the calendar together first. It shouldn't take more than five or ten minutes."

At eight-forty-five, Zeke's car pulled up to the gate. The guard had received a call from Brady and had veri-fied Goodman's name from his driver's license. Gardner listened intently to the brief conversation as he telephoned Lemoine.

"Goodman is in the complex. Tell everyone it's show time."

All four in the kitchen wore white bathrobes closed completely in the front to hide the protective vests they all wore. Samantha was a bundle of nerves, but Alex tried to calm her.

"What am I doing here, Alex? I've seen the guy. I know it's him in my dreams, and I've passed this onto others. So, what more can I do?"

"Stay calm. I'm here too, and I don't think I was anybody else in another life. We'll be going home soon."

"But I'm wearing a god-damned bullet proof vest, Alex, and so are you. The curtains from the sliders behind us are wide open, and it's pitch dark outside. Talk about easy targets."

Mike looked sympathetically at Samantha, touched her right hand on the table they sat at, and smiled.

"Samantha, you even sound like Susan when you complain. Part of me wants you to keep telling me more about her as you see her, but another part of me knows how you must feel living the lives of two people. I hope Susan sets you free sometime soon. I don't know how we'd have gotten this far without you."

As she rose from her chair to pour herself a glass of wine from the open bottle on the kitchen counter, the sound of gunfire startled her. The glass sliders shattered as all four of them dove to the floor. Samantha quickly reached for the light switch on the wall behind the wine bottle, and the room suddenly was pitch black. Then, in a split second, spotlights in the back yard went on and they all could see a figure darting across the yard behind the property next door. Ed Lemoine ran down the stairs toward the kitchen and yelled.

"Is everyone okay? Stay down."

Mike scanned the room and yelled, "Bonnie, Alex, Samantha, are you okay?" One by one they answered they were. Alex held Samantha tightly as she shivered uncontrollably.

Lemoine's phone rang. "Ed, he's on foot, heading behind the houses where it's dark and no street lights. He must have parked his car on another street. Stay put with everyone. Call the guard station. Make sure they don't open the gate for anyone until I get there. I'll see if I can pick up his movement."

Lemoine quickly had all four crawling on the floor toward the stairs. He followed them upstairs into the master bedroom and told them to close and lock the door. He then called the guard station as he hid behind the railing at the top of the stairs, waiting in silence.

Gardner drove his car slowly from street to street with his headlights off. As he rounded the corner from Cranmore onto Dawes, he spotted the Mercedes parked a short distance away. He stopped his car and waited. Suddenly, the tail lights of the Mercedes blinked twice and Gardner knew Goodman was near. He slumped in his car trying not to be seen. His was the only other vehicle on the street. Goodman noticed the car which had not been there when he first arrived. He retraced his path behind one of the houses and walked toward the front of a house on Cranmore, behind Gardner's car. He could see Gardner on the driver's side. He quietly crossed the street moving stealthily behind some other houses. The cover of darkness made it easy for him to move from house to house.

He managed to rid himself of the gun he carried by dumping it into a recycle bin at the curb of one of the houses, being certain to wipe his prints off the gun first. He soon reached 1200 Dawes and rang the doorbell.

"Hi, Zeke, come on in," yelled Ernie Brady.

"Hi, Ernie, I had trouble reading the house numbers, so I ended up parking down the street and walked."

"Oh, I'm sorry, Zeke. I didn't think it was dark enough yet for the outside lights."

"No problem, Ernie. Listen, I don't think I'll need to change your schedule after all this week. I think we have all the coverage we need. I could use a beer, if you've got one."

Zeke stayed at Brady's for twenty minutes and then left as he walked toward his car. Gardner jumped out of the police car, drew his gun, and walked toward him.

"Hands where I can see them, Goodman. Put your hands on the roof of the car. You know the drill."

"Detective Gardner, what's going on here?"

"Shooting at people is still a crime, even in Florida, Goodman."

"I haven't the slightest idea what you're talking about, detective. I've just been visiting a co-worker."

Following a thorough body search, and a search of his Mercedes, Gardner was miffed. He called Lemoine and said he would be at the house shortly with Goodman under custody. He handcuffed Goodman and placed him in the back seat of his car, and drove the short distance to Mike's house. All the lights in the house were now lit and Lemoine had opened the front door when Goodman arrived. He escorted Goodman in the house and plopped him on a sofa in the living room. He then called Lemoine aside just outside the open front door and they conferred about what they would do next.

In the meantime, Samantha and Alex were the first two to come down the staircase from the bedroom upstairs. She stared at Goodman on the sofa as he smiled their way.

"You think you're clever, don't you, preying on innocent women who can't defend themselves. Susan Strange let you in her house and you shamelessly shot her three times. I'll never forget your face, you piece of shit," Samantha yelled at Goodman as her anger went wild.

"Have we met before? I don't recall the face," Goodman replied with a smirk on his face.

"We've met hundreds of times over the years. I've waited for this day for a long, long time."

"I'm sorry, but I haven't the faintest idea who you are."

CHAPTER 38

The police cruiser arrived at Mike's house within minutes of Gardner's call. A second car arrived a few minutes later. Gardner instructed the patrolmen to search behind each house on both streets. The four patrolmen, using their flashlights, began combing the area looking for the gun used in the shooting.

Shortly later, a forensic team arrived on the scene and began extracting bullets from various parts of the kitchen. One was found directly in the wall, about seven feet up. Another was found in the lower wall section in the family room adjacent to the open kitchen area. The forensic team met with Gardner and had worried looks on their faces.

"Based on the trajectory of the bullets we located so far, detective, it doesn't appear as if the shooter was aiming at anybody sitting at this table, or he was an incredibly bad shot. None of the angles come close to the table where these people were sitting. Looks to us like somebody was giving these people a warning here."

Gardner walked out the doorway, shattered glass crumbling under his feet, and faced the screen fencing surrounding the pool area. He made his way to the back yard beyond the fencing, and flashed his light on the ground near the bullet holes in the screen. In the grass below the holes, he found four shell casings from a nine millimeter revolver.

"Ed, this Goodman's pretty clever. There's no trace of a gun, we checked his alibi at his buddy's house, and I don't think we have enough on him to keep him locked up overnight."

Gardner looked back inside the house and could see Samantha walking toward Goodman on the sofa. His hands were handcuffed behind his back, and a patrolman stood by watching him.

"I remember you that day, the innocent cable guy checking on bad reception in the neighborhood. You were so polite in your little hard hat with Venture written on it. What did I ever do to you to deserve three bullets I never expected? You thought I was dead, didn't you? Well, here I am asshole. It took me a long time to get to this moment, but let's see if you can bullshit your way out of this one. When you poured yourself a drink and left the glass on the counter, I'll bet you thought you were pretty smart in wiping your prints. Guess what, you didn't wipe the rim, and you left your DNA on the glass, and the police still have the glass, all nice and sealed. When they match the DNA to you, let's see who's so smart then," Samantha blurted out in a rage.

Goodman's face suddenly dropped and the smirk on his face disappeared.

"Who are you? I've never seen you before."

Samantha moved closer to Goodman, standing but a few feet from his seat on the sofa. The patrolman walked toward her and told her not to go any closer.

"Look at me. Look very close. I'm not afraid of you. You can't hurt me anymore. Susan Strange is not afraid of you. Do you understand?"

Mike, Bonnie, and Alex watched in amazement as Samantha's ranting went on. She bet that Goodman did not remember Susan's face after all these years. The worried look on his face told it all.

"You can't prove a thing against me, lady. I want a lawyer. I'm not saying a thing until I get a lawyer."

Gardner heard the conversation and approached Goodman.

"Book him for attempted murder. When he gets to the station, see if there are any powder burns on his hands from the gun. And we will find the gun, Mr. Goodman. Get this guy out of here and down to the station now."

Alex rushed to Samantha and took her in his arms. She was now trembling again, as if she was coming out of a freezer at some meat shop. She began to cry until she regained her composure a few minutes later. Mike and Bonnie came to her as well.

"Wow, what a performance. You even had me believing you were Susan just now. What hell this must have been for Susan to have her life end like this. It's bothered me all these years, but never more than just now. Oh, Samantha, I hope she sets you free soon," Mike said with tears in his eyes. "It's time for you to go home. There's nothing more you can do."

At eleven o'clock, all the policemen and forensic people were preparing to leave when a patrolman walked in with a gun in a plastic bag.

"This might be what you were looking for, detective."

"Where did you find it?" Gardner asked.

"In a recycling barrel down the street. I don't know if there are prints on the gun, sir, but this gun's definitely been fired lately. I could smell it from the barrel."

Two of the patrolmen covered the broken glass sliders with plastic sheets and taped it closed. The entire perimeter of the house was roped off and two patrolmen were assigned in front of the house for the rest of the evening. Gardner and Lemoine would be back in the morning to review the tapes in the upstairs bedroom.

The two couples grabbed some of their personal belongings and were escorted to a nearby hotel for the night. Once Samantha entered the hotel room with Alex, she tossed her bag down and plopped herself down in the lounge chair near the bed.

"I've had enough, Alex. I want to go home tomorrow."

As soon as she was ready for bed, she held Alex tightly and said.

"I don't know how I could have done this without you. I love you, Alex Brien, and thank you for being here for me."

There were no dreams waking her this night, no nightmares, and no faces of a tattooed man with a scar on his chin to torment her. The demons were finally gone.

CHAPTER 39

The next morning, Goodman had a lawyer to represent him. Marsha had called her father, and he made arrangements for Zeke to have an attorney at the station posting bail, if necessary.

Gardner and Lemoine did not have direct evidence of Goodman at the crime scene, nor were there powder fragments on his hands. Gardner assumed he wore gloves. But again, the police had no proof linking Goodman at the house. He was released, but told not to leave Orlando until further notice. At around noon, Marsha drove Zeke to his car at the police impound lot, and said she would see him back at their house.

Zeke retrieved the keys to his Mercedes from the parking attendant at the impound after handing him the necessary release papers from the police station. He placed the key in the ignition, and as he turned the key, the car exploded violently, and all you could see was a ball of fire. Marsha heard the explosion from several hundred yards down the road, and a smirk appeared on her face. She kept on driving toward Lakeview Terrace, knowing fully Zeke would not be home for dinner. She picked up her cellphone and made a call.

"So much for the Mercedes. I'll be mourning for a few days. Why don't you stop in on Saturday? I don't think I'll be taking a tennis lesson this weekend."

She hung up the phone and drove home. When she arrived, she tossed her car keys on the kitchen counter and walked to the bedroom. She stood on a desk chair near the bed and reached for the air-conditioning ceiling vent above. She unsnapped the vent and removed the camera from inside. She then opened her laptop, grabbed a USB adaptor, and plugged her camera into the computer. A picture appeared on her screen of the painting which hid Zeke's wall safe. The angle of the camera focused directly on the combination of the safe when the door was open.

Marsha continued to run the video as she started to write down numbers on a pad while observing Zeke opening the safe on the video. When Zeke turned the lever and the safe opened, Marsha stopped the video. She rose from the computer station and walked to the wall safe. One by one, she spun the tumblers very deliberately and opened the safe.

The safe contained nearly three hundred thousand dollars. She quickly stashed the money in a large leather pocketbook, closed the safe, and wiped it clean of any fingerprints. She then deleted the video from the computer and her camera, and removed the memory card from the camera. Then she replaced the air-conditioning vent, got in her car, and drove to the fitness center in the complex. Once she arrived, she went straight for the lockers in the ladies locker room. With no one in sight, she unlocked one of the small lockers, inserted the purse, and re-locked the locker, taking the key with her for locker fifty-four. She then headed for one of the treadmills in the exercise room and began jogging. She had a smile on her face as she spoke.

"So long, asshole. Let's see who has the last laugh now."

Within thirty minutes, Gardner entered the fitness center after finding out what Marsha's car looked like. She was still on the treadmill, soaking in sweat, as she saw them approach. She stopped the machine, grabbed a towel, and wrapped it around her shoulders.

"Mrs. Goodman?" Gardner asked with Lemoine standing by his side. "We have some bad news."

* * *

Samantha and Alex were prepared to leave for Providence on the four-thirty Southwest flight. They were startled by a knock on their hotel room door around one o'clock.

"Sergeant Lemoine, what brings you here?"

"Apparently someone else had issues with Zeke Goodman. An hour after he was released this morning, someone blew up his car at the impound center with him inside. Goodman is dead." He looked directly at Samantha and went on.

"I hope this means he is gone from your life for good. I just left Mike's room. I think they'll be on the same flight as you to Providence this afternoon."

"Do you have any idea who might have done this?" Alex asked. Lemoine simply shook his head.

"I'm afraid this is Lieutenant Gardner's problem now. I think I can close the Susan Strange file when I get back. I don't think there's any more we can do. It'll have to stay as a cold case in the files, but I don't think Mike will be upset by it. It's been a long week, folks. Have a safe trip home."

Two minutes later, there was another knock on their door. It was Mike.

"You've heard?"

"Yes, Sergeant Lemoine just left," answered Alex.

"I have no doubt whatsoever he was responsible for Susan's death. Although he never admitted it, he was more nervous by the minute. I could see it just by looking right at him. Can you imagine, a few days ago I couldn't look at this guy in the eyes. Last night, I think I just couldn't help myself. I would have scratched out his throat if I had the chance. I hope I never see his face again," Samantha said.

"I feel like Susan's at peace finally, and so am I. Your nightmares and making me believe they existed, I don't know how I can ever repay you for all of this. Alex, never let her get away," Mike pleaded. He shook Alex by the hand and then hugged Samantha and began to cry. She understood and let the moment last.

On Friday morning, a small gathering attended Zeke Goodman's funeral as Larry Pelican held his daughter by the arm throughout the entire ceremony. The afternoon collation was held at a restaurant near the cemetery and lasted until three o'clock. Marsha told her father that she wanted to spend some time alone for a while and might go on a cruise. But for now, she wanted to go home and spend some time by herself.

On her way home, she stopped at the fitness center and retrieved her purse from the locker. She got into her bathing suit once she entered the house, grabbed a glass and a bottle of wine and headed poolside. This night she did not mind being alone.

The doorbell rang at Marsha's on Saturday at one o'clock. Marsha was scantily dressed as she opened the front door.

"I thought you'd never get here," she said.

With a bottle of champagne in one hand, and two glasses in the other, there stood Danny Scott, closing the door behind him.

* * *

Alex and Samantha graduated from Northeastern the following May and announced their wedding plans in July. Following the wedding ceremony and reception in Hoboken, they planned to relocate to Somerville, Massachusetts following their honeymoon. Alex was to become the manager of La Mâison Henri, and Samantha would begin teaching at the Brackett Elementary School in Arlington, one town over.

Their honeymoon would be in Hana, Hawaii, a two-week paid trip compliments of Mike and Bonnie Strange.

EPILOGUE

Meanwhile, in Chicago, Illinois, a son was born to Bob and Holly Jones. In a few years, the boy would begin to complain of nightmares about a young woman in a white bathrobe shouting angrily at him, and a sudden explosion in a car. It was diagnosed simply as night terrors that would eventually go away.

N O T E

Radon gas exposure is still a major cause of lung cancer among non-smokers. Too many homeowners are still unaware of the dangers posed by radon gas. Similar to colonoscopies being able to prevent cancer of the colon from occurring, radon mitigation tests and the ensuing remedial action can prevent homeowners from unnecessary exposure to radon gas, minimizing the likelihood of lung cancer in future years for the non-smoker. My sincere thanks to Peter Hendrick, Executive Director of The American Association of Radon Scientists and Technologies for his thoughtful insight on the need for mandatory radon inspections in the future.

<u>Please review this book:</u> Thank you for buying and reading *A Life Before*. I sincerely hope you enjoyed reading it. If

you did, please do a review for me on Amazon. This would remind other prospective readers why they too should read the book. Amazon reviews really help an author, and I am no different. Thank you for considering doing this. And if you haven't yet, take a look at my first two award-winning thrillers, *Flower of Heaven* and *Dangerous Bloodlines,* you won't be disappointed.

ACKNOWLEDGEMENTS

To Pauline, Barbara, David, and Julie, your copyediting and proofreading were every bit what I expected from each of you. My family continues to be my biggest supporter. To Glenn Ruga, who makes my website look like a work of art, thank you for all the hard work you and Visual Communications continually put out, and for your critique of the cover art and layout of the book. To Jennifer Givner of Acapella Book Design, you've been there for me twice now and I hope others realize your outstanding skills at designing and creating a book cover that tells a story.

73401435R00160

Made in the USA
Columbia, SC
11 July 2017